Fashionably

Deceptive

Author Tonia

The Osborne Publishing Company Presents:
Fashionably Deceptive

This novel is a work of fiction. Any resemblances to real people, living or dead, actual events, establishments, organizations, or locales are intended to give the fiction a sense of reality. Other names, characters, places, and incidents are either products of the author's imagination or are used fictitiously.

For information contact:
Tonia the Author
toniatheauthor@gmail.com

ISBN-13:
978-1484917527
ISBN-10:
1484917529
LCCN: 2013907026

www.toniatheauthor.com

Dedication

This book is dedicated to God for blessing me with this talent and to all of the individuals that have been there along this journey. I realize that I am nothing without Him and the countless others that have spent hours helping to make this project a success.

Whether you offered feedback, helped edit, or just simply gave your words of encouragement, I appreciate you from the bottom of my heart. There are far too many of you to name, considering this project began in 2007, but just know that I wouldn't be here today without you.

A special thanks goes out to Niccole at 21st Street Urban Editing for her knowledge and assistance throughout this process.

Prologue
October, 2005

The ebony beauty shivered against the cold as she lit her crack pipe. She knew the small amount she had remaining would not last, so, as the toxic smoke filled her lungs, she was already formulating a strategy to get to her next high.

Throwing her mess of long, tangled black hair over her shoulders, she adjusted her dingy designer dress, and walked barefoot to the thug standing on the corner. The fat that rolled around his waist was barely concealed under a long white tee and leather jacket. She tried to avoid the broken glass strewn about the scarcely lit street, and she now wished that she had not given up her strapless Ferragamo stilettos for her last high.

"Do you have something?" she asked as she approached him, twitching with the signature itch her craving was known to cause.

"Bitch, do you have some money this time?" the boy asked as he turned up his nose to drown out the stench, which now clung to her skin after spending too many hours in a crack house.

"N-No," she stammered as she turned her stained pocketbook upside down, and rummaged about her once elegant designer dress.

"Well, what you gon' do for this shit then?" he asked as he leered at the once priceless dime piece and flashed a mouthful of yellow gold.

If he'd had a heart, he would have felt pity. Instead, all he felt was aroused as he looked her up and down. It seemed like, just yesterday, he used to watch her around town, and she wouldn't even glance his way. Now, he had what she needed.

Following him into a nearby alley, rank with the smell of piss, she tried to fight back the tears. *When and how did this thing get this out of control?*

As the keeper of her next high led her behind a rancid dumpster, she wiped her eyes with the back of her hand. *Now is not the time to cry.* She bent over, clutched the dumpster with her bare hands, and bit her lip as the street corner thug grabbed her hair, lowered his sweats, and entered her roughly from behind.

As he pumped his fully erect six inches in and out of her, she struggled not to vomit.

"Oooh, this shit good..." he moaned. "Tell me, this is not the best dick your uppity ass ever had. You know you been wanting this shit," he added as sweat poured from his bald head and down his chubby face.

It didn't take long for him to cum, and as he ejaculated, he didn't even bother to pull out. As far as he was concerned, she hadn't been in the streets long enough to have something, and a baby would be her problem. As cum slowly trickled down her leg, she knew she had reached her all-time low.

"Turn around, bitch, 'cause you about to give me head," he grunted as he snatched her by her neck and forced her to her knees.

He held her head down as she placed his slimy dick, now coated with her own vaginal juices, into her mouth. There was no turning back at this point. He pounded in and out of her mouth with untamed fury, while she just prayed that he would hurry up and finish. She would need the high now more than ever.

Chapter 1
Fall, 2007

"Dareon! If you don't open this damn door, I swear, I will kick this shit in."

Kayla beat on Dareon's door. First with one fist and then with two, alternating between screaming out obscenities and pacing the hallway of his six-figure condominium.

I am so tired of his cheating black ass. It has been three long years, and this nigga still has not changed. Same shit, different day.

"Dareon, open the door! I know you have a bitch in there. You're gonna make me kick both of y'all's asses."

Just as Kayla raised her fist to continue her assault on the door, it opened to reveal Dareon, wearing nothing but a pair of grey Nike shorts. He was 6'2, chocolate brown, and cut like a damn diamond. Dareon knew he was fine. Kayla scrunched her face up at her supposed-to-be boyfriend and stepped back to analyze the situation.

"What's up, bae? Why you coming over here acting like that? You know I got neighbors and shit," Dareon said nonchalantly, looking at Kayla up and down to check out the sweats she thought she had worn to come kick his ass in. "Bring your ass in the house and stop tripping."

Kayla pushed her way past Dareon as she checked out the surroundings. *Something did not feel right. It does not take anyone innocent fifteen minutes to answer the door*, she thought.

"What were you doing, Dareon? And don't lie," Kayla demanded accusingly, her arms crossed in front of her chest, a threat in her eyes.

"Kayla, I was lying down. You know I had practice all day and shit. Damn! You always come over here with this drama shit. Can a nigga just chill?"

"Whatever, Dareon. I know better than that. But fuck it, I swear I am about to break up with your ass. Jordan and Pharris keep warning me—"

"Fuck both them single-ass bitches," Dareon interjected.

Kayla sighed and plopped down on the nearby leather sectional. She gave up because she knew that arguing with Dareon was pointless, as always. Unless she had proof, she knew that he would just talk circles around her until she felt crazy for even making unsubstantiated accusations. Dareon had been blessed with a serious mouthpiece that would probably make him one hell of a litigator, if, for some reason, he didn't go pro. It only took seconds for him to join her and wrap her in his massive arms. As she leaned back into his muscular frame and tried to remain unresponsive, Kayla felt her defensive wall slowly coming down.

"Stop always thinking the worst of every situation. You know you're my girl," he murmured cajolingly into her ear, his breath hot and sweet against her neck.

Kayla had heard those words from his lips so many times, and each time she hoped that he actually meant it. She was still fuming on the inside, but decided to put her inhibitions to the side to keep the peace. She didn't resist when Dareon went from planting kisses on her face to nibbling on her neck. Fighting him off was useless; he knew exactly what he wanted and could usually figure out how to get it.

"You know I love you, right?" Dareon whispered softly. "Why can't you just trust me, and let the past and all the bullshit that you hear go? You are going to be my wife, Kayla. Stop tripping and worrying about these other hos so much. I only want your crazy ass."

The words rolling off of his tongue sounded so good, but Kayla knew that words were just words. She had been through too much with Dareon, and it was beginning to take its toll. It was possible that, for once, he wasn't being deceitful, but it was also possible that he was up to no good, per the norm. Kayla sighed and rolled out from under the comfortable familiarity of Dareon's arms and the softness of his lips. Her vision was clouded, and she needed to splash some cold water on her face.

She was oblivious to the expression that crossed Dareon's face as she entered the guest bathroom. All that Kayla could think about was regrouping. She flicked on the light, and everything went black. Crouched down in the tub, wearing nothing but a frown plastered across her face, was her worst fear manifested: a groupie ho.

****

"Hello?" Pharris answered the phone, half-delirious and confused.

Glancing at her illuminated clock, she could see that it was three A.M. *What the fuck?* Her state of delirium was short lived, though, and in mere seconds, she was out of her bed and down the hallway.

"Jordan, wake up! Kay is in jail, and we need to go downtown and pick her up now. She said something about a fight, a groupie, and Dareon's bitch ass."

"Wait! What?" Jordan asked as she tilted her head to the side and sighed exasperatedly. *This crazy bitch…*

Within minutes of receiving Kayla's phone call, her two roommates were halfway down the six flights of stairs that led to the parking garage of their loft apartment. Neither could focus as they rushed past the elevators to get to their roommate.

Pharris hit the automatic start on her BMW 750, and Jordan jumped into the passenger side. While Pharris set the navigation system, Jordan, ever mindful of her comfort, adjusted the temperature and heated the seats. It was the least she could do to take the chill out of the air. Kayla and Dareon had had their share of arguments, but neither Pharris nor Jordan could believe that things had reached this point. Jordan and Pharris didn't have much to say on the ride to the parish jail, but the solemn silence spoke volumes. Kayla had too much to lose to risk throwing it away for an unfaithful man.

****

I can't believe this shit. I went to jail, and all because this dumb-ass nigga can't keep his dick in his pants. If the police wouldn't have pulled me off that groupie bitch, I would still be getting in her ass. And Dareon…wait till I get my hands on him.

Kayla sat in the backseat of Pharris' BMW as her roommates aggravated her with their bitter complaining about being awakened in the middle of the night. *It wasn't like I had planned to go to jail. Shit happens.*

"Can we talk about something else please? And can I use one of y'all's phones to call Dareon? I think I left my cell at his house."

Jordan tossed her phone in the backseat, but not before rolling her eyes to notify Kayla that she was just about fed up. Kayla didn't even glance at her as she quickly dialed Dareon's cell.

"Where the fuck are you?"

"Man, what's up?"

"I am about to come get my shit, and you know I am not through with your ass. Where the fuck do you get off hiding some little jump off—"

Click.

"Hello! Hello?" Kayla screamed, even though Dareon had clearly connected her with the dial tone.

Too pissed off and fed up to do anything else, Kayla put her head in her lap and let the tears cascade down her face.

"I am so tired of his ass. Why do I always end up with the dog-ass niggas? I dress my ass off. I drive a Benz. My hair and nails and shit are always on point. I have my own cash, and I cut for a nigga. Why me?" Kayla sobbed loudly.

The words of consolation that her roommates threw at her did little to assuage the pain of the gaping hole in her heart. *How could this nigga be so heartless?*

Before Pharris could remove her key from the ignition, Kayla was sprinting towards her E350. *Good thing I caught campus transit to Dareon's earlier or my car would still be at his house.*

Neither Pharris nor Jordan said a word as they walked to the elevator. They both lived by the same motto: "Let Kayla do Kayla". It was a known fact that Kayla was one of those high-strung individuals who would do what she wanted, when she wanted, regardless of the consequence or lack of propriety. All that her girls could do was be there when they were needed, and, of course, throw in their opinions from time to time, even though they usually fell upon deaf ears. As far as Kayla was concerned, since neither Jordan nor Pharris had ever been in love, there was only so much advice that they could give.

Kayla sped to Dareon's house and made it there in record time. This time, she didn't even have to knock. When she got to the door, Dareon was already standing there waiting. He knew his girl as well as he knew his football plays and was only surprised it took her so long to show up. Her shoulder-length, bronze-highlighted hair was in disarray, and her hazel eyes were swollen from crying, but Kayla still looked damn good. Dareon couldn't help but notice as his dick swelled up a notch. *Damn, she even looks good when she's mad*, he thought appreciatively as he waited for the cursing out that he was sure was coming. Instead, Kayla just grabbed her phone from off the counter where she'd left it and attempted to head back out the front door.

Before she could step a foot into the hallway, Dareon grabbed her arm and pulled her back inside.

"Bae, I know you want to talk. Go ahead and say what's on your mind."

"You already know what's up, D. I am so tired of this shit. Look at what you are willing to give up for these skank-ass bitches, whose only goal in life is to get knocked up by someone about to go pro. I love you, but damn! How much can a bitch take? And why didn't you come bail me out, or, better yet, why did you call the police?"

"I didn't call anybody. You know I don't roll like that. But with the way you were handing it to ol' girl, one of the neighbors probably called. And you know I was gon' come get you out, but I just had to work out some things here first."

"What's more important than bailing your girl out, D?" Kayla asked unbelievingly, rolling her eyes. She knew bullshit when she heard it. In the words of Trina, "*Blah, blah, blah*."

"Just tell me how much I owe your girls, and I will give them their—"

"This is not about money, Dareon," Kayla interrupted. "My girls got me. The point is you were not there, like always. You think you can just throw out some cash, and that will make all of our problems go away. I am not some ghetto bitch. Did you forget that my mom is an attorney, and my dad owns one of the top landscaping companies in Texas? What the fuck is wrong with you, Dareon?"

Tired of arguing and ready to lay it down, because he knew his coach would have him doing two-a-days if he was late for practice, Dareon lowered his head in defeat and let a single tear fall down his face. *The tears always get 'em.*

Sure enough, before long he was in the bed next to Kayla sound asleep, but not before getting the make-up pussy he knew was reserved only for him, no matter how many times he fucked up.

Chapter 2

Kayla sat in her apartment and tried to study, but, no matter how hard she tried to concentrate, she could not stop thinking about how dissatisfied she was with her life. One semester away from graduating at the top of her class with a bachelor's degree in criminal justice, and all she could think about was how she was going to get away from this fucked up thing called love. Realizing that she was not going to get any studying done, she closed her books. Then, she closed her eyes. *Might as well take a quick nap before the girls get home.*

As soon as she had fallen into a deep sleep, her cell phone rang off the hook. *Here we go. Here we go again.* Kayla answered her phone before Trina could finish her interlude.

"Hello?" Kayla answered in her best "I am trying to sound awake, but am clearly knocked out" voice.

"Bae, let's go to the movies. Get dressed. I will be there to pick you up in an hour."

"But, Dareon, I have to study."

Dareon hung up before Kayla could even finish her sentence. Surrendering, she got up and took a quick shower. Knowing that Dareon was always on time, except for when he was out fucking up, Kayla threw open her walk in closet to get jazzy for her man. After selecting a pair of grey Christian Dior skinny jeans and a sheer black Christian Dior top, Kayla threw her ensemble on the bed.

She rubbed Bath & Body Works' Japanese Cherry Blossom lotion on her smooth skin before throwing on a Victoria's Secret Embrace bra to enhance her small, but perky chest. She curled a few strands of hair before getting dressed, and just as she was slipping on her Louboutin stilettos, Dareon sent her a text to inform her that he was downstairs.

Standing in front of her mirror, Kayla looked herself up and down. At 5'3 and 120 pounds, Kayla was slim and fine, with an ass that most bitches couldn't compete with. She was bad, and she knew it, even though with the twists and turns that her love life took, you would swear she was clinging on to the only man she would ever get. After misting on a light spray of Dareon's favorite Bond No. 9 perfume, Kayla grabbed her black Fendi spy bag and walked to the elevator.

The black Escalade on black and chrome twenty-four inch rims was parked by the elevator with Dareon waiting, relaxed, in the driver's seat. When she hopped in the SUV, she quickly gave him a peck on the lips. Then, she leaned back to inspect his appearance. Dareon was trendy, as usual, in a pair of True Religion jeans that fell on his waist in the perfect place, a fitted white tee that exposed the lithe muscles underneath, and, of course, the latest Jordans.

The average person would never have assumed that Dareon was already a multi-millionaire. His dad had passed when he was younger but had left the family set for life with vast investments and a lucrative partnership in one of the top law firms in the country.

Kayla absorbed his entire physique and took in his jewelry, from the glistening earrings in both ears to his signature presidential Rolex. She couldn't help but smile to herself and think, *Damn! He looks good.*

As Dareon headed out of her complex and into traffic, she leaned back in the plush leather seat, inhaled his cologne, and let the sounds of Robin Thicke soothe her as they headed to the Rave movie theatre to catch *Déjà Vu* starring Denzel Washington. It was times like these that she loved him most. No words were needed. They could just ride in silence and let the sounds from the satellite radio system do the talking for them…*I am lost without you, can't help myself…*

****

After the movie, Dareon dropped Kayla off at her place, so she could finish studying. Even though she sensed that he was too eager to drop her back off at home, instead of trying to stay over for a nightcap, she dismissed the feeling and raced upstairs to tell her girls about Denzel's fine ass. If there was one older man that Kayla loved, it was some Denzel.

As soon as she hit the front door, she could hear music playing and laughter. *The girls are in full effect tonight. I guess I won't get any studying done,* Kayla thought resignedly as she entered the large living area of their loft. Before long, she was engulfed in laughter with Jordan and Pharris, forgetting all about studying for the exam she had in a few days. Between talks of Kayla having to beat down the groupie chick, who had been identified as some jump-off named Samara, and the upcoming Kappa party that Saturday, the girls cut up till well after two A.M.

Finally exhausted, all three girls went to their separate bedrooms. After showering and before drifting off into a deep slumber, Kayla dialed Dareon.

You know who you have reached. Leave a message, and I will hit you back.

The phone went straight to voicemail. The nagging insecurity she felt from earlier was gnawing at her again. She contemplated whether she should be suspicious or let the issue go. After choosing the latter, she rolled over and drifted off into a deep sleep. She hadn't talked to him since he'd dropped her off after the movie. *But, sometimes, you have to make yourself think everything is just fine, even if it's just for the sake of a good night's sleep.*

****

The sound of her alarm forced her awake, so Kayla rolled out of bed and groggily stepped into her restroom to handle the morning essentials: brushing her teeth, washing her face, applying scented lotion to her skin. She, then, stepped into her closet to choose her outfit for class. Today was Friday, the last day of the school week, the day she always chose to flaunt her urban wear. Kayla quickly chose a black and white House of Dereon hooded dress that she'd purchased from the Galleria in Houston on her last visit home, and a recently purchased pair of Christian Louboutin patent peep toe stilettos.

She only had one class on Fridays from 10 to 11, and the rest of the day was usually spent running errands that she could not get to during the week. After dressing and unwrapping her hair, she applied a light coat of DKNY Be Delicious perfume and glossed her lips with her new Florabundance lip glass from M·A·C. She grabbed her Fendi spy bag, rocking it again since it matched today's ensemble, her school books, and quickly headed out the door. Professor Mure was known for embarrassing students who came in late to his class, and she would've hated to have to check his ass, again. It was only 9:30, but she knew she'd better leave early. Parking was a bitch at Louisiana State University.

After circling the parking lot repeatedly, Kayla finally saw a black Civic coming out of a spot two rows ahead. She zipped through the lot to get to the parking spot and almost hit a black Escalade cutting through to get to Highland Street. For a second, she thought it was Dareon's truck, but, when she noticed the blonde girl driving, she quickly dismissed the notion. And with all the black Escalades that prowled LSU's vast campus, Kayla failed to give the vehicle a second thought. In her haste, she did not take notice of the Texas license plate.

After class, she decided to stop in on her baby to see what he was doing. He didn't have class on Fridays, and it was not yet time for football practice. And, on top of that, she had not talked to him since the movies, nor had he returned any of her numerous text messages.

She stopped by Subway to pick up two subs, one for her and one for Dareon, then drove her Benz towards the condos where Dareon lived. She parked in a visitor's spot and rode the elevator to his floor. She couldn't wait to see the expression on Dareon's face when he saw how good she looked. He loved seeing her in dresses. And maybe after he ate his sub, he would be ready for dessert, he always said her pussy was like a drug to him.

When Kayla knocked, Dareon answered the door wearing a white wife beater and grey sweats. Giving him the once over, she brushed past him and strutted into his condo, making sure her ass sashayed slightly as she headed toward the bar to eat. Her sway didn't go unnoticed as Dareon grabbed his dick and walked over to the bar to join her. *She better not have on any panties on under that dress 'cause she's next on the menu,* Dareon thought, smirking to himself.

"What's so funny?" Kayla asked coyly, noticing the smirk.

"Nothing, Bae, just thinking that you wearing the fuck out that dress, and thinking about what you gon' look like without it in a few minutes," he teased.

Kayla pretended to dismiss the comment with a wave of her hand as they sat down to eat and chatted blithely about their plans for the day. However, she couldn't help but notice the way the muscles in Dareon's arms bulged as he picked at his sandwich, and the warmth his words brought to the area below her abdomen. *This nigga knows that he is sexy as hell. Fresh haircut, perfect white teeth, long eyelashes that curve just slightly, muscles in all the right places from numerous football practices and spring trainings, and a nine inch dick accompanied by a hurricane tongue.* Kayla snuck glances at him as they ate. Even after three years, his appearance could still turn her on. She was so transfixed by his good looks that she didn't even notice him slowly reaching under the bar and beneath her dress to explore the hidden treasures underneath. *No panties. Just the way I like it,* Dareon thought as he spread her lower lips and began to work on massaging her clit.

Kayla spread her legs obligingly as Dareon massaged her spot with his fingers. Putting down her sandwich, she leaned her head back and moaned as he worked his magic, alternating between using two and three fingers to work her to an orgasm. Before she knew it, Dareon lifted her atop the bar, and replaced his fingers with the swirling magic of his tongue. Both of them moaned in satisfaction. Kayla for the feelings of pleasure Dareon created as he licked and sucked her clit, and Dareon because there was nothing he loved more than the taste of pussy. Kayla began to shudder as she coated Dareon's tongue with the fruits of his labor.

Dareon pulled Kayla from the bar, as she kissed and licked her juices from his face. Knowing that there was more to come, she pulled Dareon towards the master bedroom. After she unzipped her dress, she pulled down his sweats and boxers as he lifted his wife beater over his head. She pushed him roughly onto the king size bed, and straddled him, slowly riding his dick as she held onto the headboard. Dareon grabbed her hips and began thrusting deep into her, keeping the slow pace they both liked so much. Picking up speed, Kayla clutched the headboard tighter and rode all nine thick inches of Dareon until she felt him tense up. When she felt him begin to go soft, she released the second orgasm she had held in until he got his.

Never a selfish lover, Kayla waited until Dareon had completely released his semen into her before she replaced her pussy with her mouth and sucked Dareon back into action. A master at what she was doing, Kayla sucked Dareon's thick member until he couldn't take anymore. Turning Kayla over onto her stomach, Dareon eased inside her tight walls and hit it from the back until they reached orgasm again. It would be two hours before she headed back to her vehicle, and to her house to take a hot shower. No matter how Dareon begged for her to stay and shower at his place, his bathrooms still held a fucked up memory.

Chapter 3

Kayla was in love. So much so that her heart hurt every time she thought about Dareon. And no matter how bad he was for her, she could not leave him alone. Even when she got the courage to leave, he would always come back to her door, begging. To Kayla, finding a good younger black man was like making a one night stand pay child support…when all you knew was his nickname. *It hurts when you think that you have someone who will cherish you and is in it for the long haul, only to find out that the long haul to them means as long as things are going their way.* Dareon was Kayla's life, and had been since they'd hooked up during her freshman year in college.

Kayla met Dareon after a football game at a local bar called Fred's. She was usually not into hanging out at bars crawling with football players and groupies, but Kayla had let Pharris and Jordan talk her into going only because she needed a break after a strenuous week of midterm exams. From the moment she hit the door, plainly clad in Seven jeans and a simple purple Prada tunic with matching purple peep-toe flats, it was pandemonium. Random guys approached the crew from every angle to either buy drinks or get in a quick dance. But in between dancing and sipping free drinks, the girls pretty much avoided all the guys who approached them, at least, until Dareon approached Kayla.

The minute he approached her and she looked into those hazel bedroom eyes and saw those perfect white teeth, she was like a giddy preteen girl. They ended up outside in his truck, talking and laughing like old friends. Little did she know that this guy, who came off as being so sweet and caring, was really a whore sent from the realms below. She ignored all the warning signs and advice from those who knew Dareon, and, before long, Kayla was head over heels in love. She was like Kanye West— you couldn't tell her nothing.

After showering, reapplying lip gloss, and changing into a very fashionable pink Juicy Couture bubble bottom dress and a pair of gold Vera Wang stilettos, she headed out the door and into traffic for a day of errand running. Dareon had made sure that he temporarily ruined her House of Dereon dress during their midday sex session, but she didn't mind because dressing up was her thing. She had to drop several suits and various other clothing items off at the cleaners for both her and Dareon before going to her weekly appointments with both her hair dresser and manicurist. If she had time after her errands, she wanted to shoot to New Orleans for a quick shopping spree at Lakeside Mall.

Shopping in Baton Rouge was cruel and unusual punishment, and, if she didn't make it to New Orleans, she would be stuck having to find an outfit for the Kappa party at the tiny Bebe in the Mall of Louisiana.

As fate would have it, Kayla didn't leave the hair salon until well after 7:30 P.M. Her hairdresser, Mia, was one of the best in Baton Rouge, but— Damn!— that girl was slow. Between trying to catch up on gossip and two to three smoke breaks per hour, a trip to the hairdresser could be an all day routine. Knowing that Saturday she would want to sleep in before Dareon's football game and the Kappa fraternity party, Kayla eased her car onto I-10 and made her way toward the Mall of Louisiana.

Of course, the mall was packed. It was the weekend, and everyone had been looking forward to this Kappa party since fliers had started circulating weeks earlier. There was nothing like a fraternity or sorority party to stir up mass excitement across campus.

Kayla parked by the food court, and hurried her way into the mall and down the escalator into Bebe. Before she arrived, she called her girls to have them meet her, but thanks to traffic, she was sure they had beat her there and had probably already picked out their outfits, too.

Almost as soon as Kayla walked into the store, Jordan and Pharris waved her over to the dressing room. Both of them were modeling A-line pencil skirts in different colors with blouses to match their coordinating skirts. Kayla issued out the compliments due, and left them to try and find her outfit before the mall closed, which left her only forty-five minutes. Kayla skimmed the racks of the small store, before finally deciding on a black body conscious dress that stopped at her knees and a red waist belt with a unique crocodile pattern. Her roommates waited patiently as Kayla checked out at the nearest register, swiping Dareon's black American Express card to pay her unusually small bill of $219.88. She was sure Dareon would appreciate the measure since he was used to her shopping sprees, which easily totaled a couple of thousand for a couple of outfits.

Kayla, Jordan, and Pharris walked out of the mall together, but separated in the parking lot to go to their respective cars. Just as Kayla eased her car into drive, her phone began to ring.

"What's up, Bae. Where are you?" Dareon asked.

"Leaving the mall, you know I had to find a fit for the Kappa party tomorrow. You still not going?"

"You know I don't care much for those pretty-ass niggas. You 'bout to stop through here?"

"Aren't you supposed to be with the team? Coach is going to kick your ass," Kayla tsked. "But I guess I am on my way."

After they hung up the phone, Kayla changed direction and headed to his house. Now, she was sure that she would be sleeping in the next day after what was promising to be a long night. Damn! She loved home games, when her man would sneak from the team's hotel room to cuddle with her. On Fridays before their Saturday home games, the football team had to meet up at the field house, and would spend the night locked in a local hotel to seclude them from any disturbances. But Dareon usually found a way out of the hotel and back to his condo to be with Kayla.

****

Dareon rolled out from under Kayla as he heard his phone repeatedly vibrating against the nightstand. Glad that Kayla was a heavy sleeper, he unplugged the phone from the charger and walked into the living room to answer this persistent early morning caller.

"What's good?"

"Nothing. What's up with you? I have been trying to reach you all night. That bitch must be over there," Samara snapped.

"That bitch just happens to be my girlfriend. You know that, and, yeah, she here. You knew how it was before you got in it, so don't call me with that bullshit. Now, like I said, what do you want?" He didn't bother to hide the impatience in his voice.

Sometimes, he couldn't understand why bitches always got in over their heads. *You never wife the piece of ass.* After blowing Samara off and powering off his phone, Dareon crept back into the bed with Kayla, wrapped his arms around her, and drifted back to sleep.

Waking up to the smell of bacon and biscuits, Dareon reached across the bed only to grasp the empty space next to him. He should have known. His baby always made him breakfast on home game days. He laid back and smiled and waited for Kayla to serve him his breakfast in bed. His girl took care of him, but she alone could never satisfy his appetite for pussy, various pussies, from various hos. Just one would never do. And as long as females allowed him to get away with the shit he was doing, why stop?

What one bitch wouldn't do, another one would. As long as real niggas stayed scarce, he would always be straight. No bitch wanted a lame, and lame, Dareon was definitely not. Shit! His pockets were deep, and, as long as he gave Kayla access to all the cash she needed to support her stupendous shopping habit and laid the dick down on a regular, he knew she wasn't going anywhere, no matter how much shit she talked. Like Dareon's dad had told him, "Let your woman talk shit, because, as long as she's still talking, you still got her. It's only when she stops reasoning and bitching, that she might be thinking about leaving. Even then, just give her a little bit of act right, and she'll keep on coming back."

Dareon felt like the king of the campus, and, tonight, when Kayla went to the Kappa party, Samara's ass would be right there sucking his dick like only a pro like her could. Even Kayla couldn't deep throat the whole nine inches. And since Samara's ass was starting to demand too much of his time, he hoped that she savored tonight, because her ass was about to be replaced.

Dareon chuckled to himself as he thought about the first time he'd met Samara. Within an hour of getting her phone number, Dareon had her ass spread out in the back of his Escalade. He had grabbed her long blonde tracks and hit her from the back only moments after the head job she had gratefully given. Dareon had her screaming his name and talking in gibberish. And to think, this bitch thought she stood a chance of being his gal. All that she had ever gotten out of their arrangement was a mouthful of cum and, maybe, a burger or two.

Kayla dropped Dareon back off at the hotel around ten A.M., and watched until one of his teammates came and let him in through a back door to avoid any detection by the coaches. As soon as Dareon was safely inside the hotel, Kayla headed back down the interstate to her apartment to go back to sleep. She was bone tired after making love to Dareon all night, and she felt drained from a lack of sleep. She had woken up extra early to prepare breakfast for her baby, because she knew how he liked to eat on game days.

Kayla slept until well into the afternoon. She only woke up because her cell phone would not stop ringing. She drowned the noise out for as long as she could, but this caller would not give up. Kayla was usually not one to answer blocked numbers, but something in her gut told her that she might want to hear whatever had this caller blowing up her phone.

"Hello. Who the hell is this?" Kayla's irritation seeped through the receiver.

"Samara, bitch, and I just want you to know, since your punk ass man ain't gon' tell you, I am six weeks pregnant."

"Bitch, don't call my phone with that shit. You better call that nigga. And, if you ever call this phone again, I will kick your ass. Again."

Kayla slammed her phone down so hard that she cracked one of her freshly polished nails. Fuming mad, she rolled out the bed and stomped into her bathroom. She stared at her reflection in the mirror as tears ran down her face. This time, Dareon had gone too damn far.

Chapter 4

"What the fuck do you mean you are pregnant? I never fucked your ass without a rubber," Dareon said as he angrily stroked his goatee.

He was used to hos trying to throw babies on him, and usually didn't trip because he kept magnums handy, but he did remember the rubber breaking on a couple of occasions with Samara. *Damn! Kayla is gon' throw a fuckin' fit if I have a baby on her ass.* And he knew this bitch would put them people in his life as soon as she spit out the little bastard. *Hands down, Samara's ass was having an abortion.*

****

Kayla stayed locked in her room for the majority of the day, powering off her cell, and ignoring all attempts by her roommates to find out the source of her sorrow. She even missed the football game in her attempt to avoid seeing Dareon. Kayla thought about missing the Kappa party, too, until she realized she had been waiting too long for it. She was not going to let Dareon steal her sunshine. Her college years were coming to a close, and she was not going to allow her cheating boyfriend to steal her precious memories or time with her roommates.

Kayla powered on her cell and filled her large garden tub with steamy water and bubble bath. As she sprinkled in bath salt, she played her voicemails. All ten new voicemails were from Dareon. Even though he'd failed to mention Samara's pregnancy, she could hear the worry in his voice as he pleaded for her to return his calls, meaning that he knew that she knew. Instead, Kayla undressed and slipped into the water. Then, she called her voice of reason, her mother.

"Hello, beautiful. For you to be calling this late, I know something is wrong."

"It's Dareon. I love him, but I am not happy. It's something new every time I turn around. Why is love so complicated?"

"Baby, I know you love him, but Dareon is young and has a lot of growing up to do. You know how much you can take, and, when you are done, there will be nothing he can say to get you back."

Kayla chatted with her mom for another fifteen minutes before finally getting off the phone to bathe. Talking to her mom always relaxed her. Mrs. Davis had been married three times, and two of those times were to Kayla's father, whom she was currently married to.

When Kayla's parents divorced, while she was in high school, she was heartbroken. So she dealt with it the only way she knew how, by acting out. She had put her mother through hell, until, eventually, she ended up pregnant three weeks before her senior prom. Unable to identify her baby's father, because of her promiscuity, Kayla spent her pregnancy in hell, until she finally decided to have an abortion a couple of weeks before high school graduation. She calmed down after the abortion, but the animosity she had for her mother remained. Kayla faulted her mother for breaking up their happy family. She chose to completely disregard the fact that her father was a controlling drunk, prone to indiscretion.

Instead of counseling, Kayla's mother showered her with luxuries: access to her platinum cards, an E Class Mercedes for graduation, and anything else Kayla's heart desired. Her dad did the same in his quest to staunch the guilt he felt for psychologically damaging his only child. Kayla's mother tried to replace the void in her heart by marrying a family friend during Kayla's freshman year in college, but that ended in disaster and divorce. Mrs. Davis found out the hard way that it was no fun being married to a man that she didn't love.

After Kayla's mother's second divorce, she decided that it was long overdue that she repaired her relationship with her daughter. Being single at fifty with a daughter who despised you, even with a lucrative six figure salary, was hell. After months of family counseling with both parents present, Kayla was able to forgive her mother, and their bond was reinstated stronger than ever. Her dad was, also, able to accept responsibility for his actions through counseling, and he re-sought her mother's hand in marriage. Six months ago, her parents renewed their vows.

Kayla soaked in the tub, washing every portion of her body slowly and thoroughly, wishing her love for Dareon would disappear as easily as the suds that ran down her firm breasts, past her pierced belly button, and into the water below her Brazilian wax. Reluctantly, she climbed out of the tub, wrapped herself in a plush towel, and walked into her room to get dressed. As Kayla retrieved her newly purchased outfit from the closet, she felt a twinge of excitement about tonight's big party.

"Oh, so now you're through sulking, bitch?" Jordan asked sarcastically as she walked into Kayla's room without knocking, holding a cup of wine.

"Fuck you," Kayla said, laughing her off as she took the cup of wine from Jordan's hand and quickly downed half of it. After the day she'd had, a buzz was well-welcomed.

Jordan was the more outspoken of her two roommates, and Kayla had known that her moping was only going to be allowed for a short time. Jordan hated everything about Dareon and looked for chances to voice her opinion. It was hard watching one of her closest friends suffer, and Jordan couldn't wait for Kayla to find someone deserving of her love. Fully dressed but needing to style her asymmetrical bob, Jordan left Kayla's room to finish getting ready.

Kayla slipped into her dress, adjusted her waist belt and put on a pair of red peep-toe Vera Wang stilettos. She then lightly spritzed on her Juicy Couture perfume after applying her make-up and touching up her freshly styled hair. Her chipped nail did little to affect her flawless appearance, but she knew that tomorrow, she would have to get that fixed. As she sipped the remainder of Jordan's wine, she went into the living room to wait for her girls to finish getting ready. Kayla expected Jordan to be ready within the next few minutes, but Pharris was another story. Out of the three, it always took Pharris the longest to get ready for anything.

Kayla laughed out loud as Jordan yelled from her bedroom, "Pharris, you better be ready in ten, or we are leaving your ass!"

Kayla had met Jordan and Pharris at freshman orientation her first day at LSU, and the three had been thick as thieves ever since. Since Jordan and Pharris were both from New Orleans, only an hour away, she had also become close with their families over the years. Instead of making the four hour trip to Houston for some holidays and a good home cooked meal, she would often just hop in the car and head home with one of her girls. Neither of them had siblings, so they had bonded together like sisters and knew each other like the backs of their hands.

The girls headed out the door about thirty minutes later, looking like models. As some of the baddest bitches at LSU, they were sure to turn heads as soon as they hit Avoyelle's, the downtown club where the party was being held. Always late to arrive at any party, partially thanks to Pharris, the girls didn't arrive at Avoyelle's until well after midnight. The small club was packed, but the grown and sexy environment made the girls feel far less clustered together as they made their way to the bar.

"Three glasses of X-rated please," Kayla told the bartender when she finally reached the front of the bar.

"It's on me," Kayla heard a familiar voice say from behind her.

Not wanting to make a scene, Kayla let Dareon pay for the drinks and then briskly moved past him and onto the dance floor. He didn't try to stop her. He just posted up with his teammates, as they both perpetrated to keep their cool.

Kayla felt like tonight should be all about her, so she refused to let Dareon ruin it, like he had a habit of doing. As she joined her roommates in the cupid shuffle, she pushed Dareon to the deepest realms of her mind. The girls danced to just about every song that came on and made sure to keep their glasses filled with premium liquor, and, when "Crank That" by Soulja Boy came on, Kayla and her roommates prepared to put on a show. The roommates began to bust the dance to the song, oblivious to the crowd that gathered around them and bucked them up. Even in dresses and pencil skirts the girls could of easily out-danced just about any of the girls in the party. Buzzed and having a good time, Kayla didn't even notice Dareon glaring at her as she worked the dance floor.

“Man, stop making yourself look sprung. Stop worrying about Kayla’s ass. It’s too many hos in here for that shit,” Dareon’s teammate Byron commented out the blue.

He knew how Dareon rolled and couldn’t understand why he looked so glum over a bitch.

“Nigga, I ain’t trippin'… but while you over here being a private investigator and shit, go find out what’s up with that red bitch over there?” Dareon replied, getting back to his old ho-ish self.

If he couldn’t get any act right from his girl, he would have to just get some pussy from another broad. Within minutes, Byron came back to Dareon with the phone number of the slim red girl Dareon had referred to. Wearing a pair of skinny jeans with a simple tunic top, and sporting long red tracks, the girl looked Dareon up and down, batting her fake lashes. She assessed the fine package that was too shy to ask her for her phone number.

Smelling money from her position all the way across the room, Carlie looked over the designer slacks and button down, accented by the one carat diamond studs in each of his ears and the diamond watch, which glistened from his arm. Feeling her panties moisten at the mere thought of snagging a baller, Carlie caught Dareon’s gaze and signaled him to meet her out front of Avoyelle’s.

After watching shawty walk down the flight of stairs, which led to the exit of Avoyelle’s, Dareon waited a full five minutes before exiting the club behind his newest conquest, partially to avoid detection by Kayla and crew, and also to make the new girl wait. Dareon knew he would be fucking tonight, but he didn’t want this new bitch thinking he was anxious for some pussy. There was nothing like new pussy, but old pussy would always do, especially if it came to that versus a bitch thinking her shit was good enough to make this nigga sweat.

Dareon escorted Carlie to his truck, promising to bring her back downtown to pick up her beat up Civic, after they got to know each other a little better. Unwilling to spend more than a few dollars on a piece of ass, Dareon dashed down the interstate and exited at the nearest Motel 6. After checking into a room, Dareon led Carlie from the car, and, hopefully, out of her panties.

As soon as they were behind closed doors, Carlie's true personality emerged as she aggressively pushed Dareon onto the bed and straddled him, while they each probed each other's mouth with their tongues. Dareon removed her tunic top and unhooked her bra with skilled precision, all while Carlie licked and sucked on his earlobes and neck. Turned on by Carlie's aggressive behavior, Dareon's dick was so hard against his pants that he felt that, if he didn't get inside her soon, he would rupture something. Deciding to find out whether this chick had a good head game, Dareon pushed Carlie's head down low. He watched her undo his pants and pull his dick out of his boxers. Carlie devoured and sucked on Dareon's dick like she had a point to prove. Nothing turned Dareon on more than watching a ho's head bob up and down as she gave him head, especially if it was a fire-ass head job like the one he was currently on the receiving end of. Just when he felt his nut about to explode, Dareon grabbed Carlie's tracks and held her head down, as he made her swallow a mouthful of cum.

****

As Kayla exited Avoyelle's, she couldn't help but scan the club for Dareon. Not seeing him anywhere, she dismissed the nagging feeling that gnawed at her gut, and followed her girls to the car.

Chapter 5

Dareon picked up the phone and dialed Kayla on her cell for the fifth time in less than an hour.

This is Kayla, leave a message and...

Dareon slammed down the phone before her voicemail could finish. Kayla had been doing this shit for over two weeks now, and he had not talked to her since he knew Samara had called and announced her pregnancy. The last time Dareon had even seen Kayla was for that brief moment at Avoyelle's.

It was not like Dareon had not been trying. He had even gone so far as to pass by her apartment several times, hoping to catch her at home. The few times he had spotted her car, he had knocked on the door, only to be told by her snobbish roommates that she wasn't there. Fine as them bitches were, he couldn't stand either of their stuck-up asses. All they knew how to do was talk shit and try and give Kayla advice about her relationship, when both of their asses were single. And to top off Dareon's two weeks from hell, the bitch he had fucked after the Kappa party had given him crabs. Between football, Samara's crazy ass, and his recent crab infestation, Dareon was missing the hell out of Kayla.

****

Kayla sent Dareon to voicemail for what felt like the hundredth time that day. He was trippin', but still she tried to convince herself that, if he was calling, it, at least, meant that he cared. And, secretly, she missed the hell out of him. Every night that she laid in her bed alone, she would snuggle under her pillows, wishing instead she was under her man. And almost every other night, she had to stop herself from either calling him or going by his place, foolishly thinking that, since she cried with or without him, there was no point in not being with him. It was only God that was carrying her through that stage, and surprisingly things were getting easier. She could feel in her heart, that her misery was only going to be temporary, and that there was something better out there for her.

Just as Kayla eased her car into the parking garage, returning from turning in a term paper she had spent most of the night typing, her phone began to vibrate noisily in her purse. Not recognizing the number, she snatched up the phone, ready to cuss Dareon out for having the audacity to call her from another number. *Why couldn't he give her time to get her head together?*

"Hello! What do you want?" answered a very irritated Kayla.

"What has my son done now?"

Embarrassed at her harsh tone, and feeling like an ass for not recognizing Dareon's mother's number, she quickly tried to cover up for her rash reaction.

"Sorry, Ms. Nicole. I had a paper due early this morning and am extremely exhausted. Plus, I thought you were someone else."

"It's okay, Kayla, but I was just calling to make sure you were still coming to the family reunion this weekend. For some reason, Dareon has not been able to give me a straight answer on whether or not to expect you. You guys are not having problems, are you?"

Irritated, but not surprised that Dareon would indirectly involve his mother in their business, Kayla assured Ms. Nicole that she would not miss the function, and ended the call, completely disregarding the question about her relationship. Yes, she might be going, but not with Dareon's sneaky ass.

As she exited her vehicle, her phone rang again, but, before Trina could finish her lovesick tune, Kayla powered off her Treo and tossed it inside her Chloe bag.

****

"Yes, she is coming, baby, from what she told me," Dareon's mother told him within seconds of talking to Kayla.

Nicole knew Dareon must have been desperate when he called her and asked her to call Kayla. Since he was her only child, Nicole lived to make Dareon happy, even if that meant getting involved in his love affairs. She had even gone so far as to offer Samara $20,000 to have an abortion, far more than what she thought the ghetto ho was worth. In the household of Nicole Anderson, her family came first, and she would be damned if some bastard child tarnished her good family name.

Dareon had grown up in a single family home in a prosperous Dallas suburb. His dad had died of a heart attack when Dareon was young, leaving Nicole set for life with over $1 million dollars in life insurance and an inherited partnership in a multi-million dollar corporate law firm. Even though the circumstances surrounding the death of Dareon's father were questionable, Ms. Nicole and her son had worked to put the ordeal behind them and had a very strong relationship. Growing up, Dareon filled the void of not having a father with football, and, as early as his freshman year in high school, it was projected that he would be one of the top scouted wide receivers in the United States.

Exceptionally gifted, rich, and gorgeous, Dareon was a ladies' man from the time he could walk and talk. A skilled manipulator, Dareon had used women all of his life, especially in high school, to satisfy his tremendous sexual appetite. From Dareon's first penetration and taste of pussy at the age of thirteen, he had never been quite able to satisfy his desire for sex. A certified nympho, Dareon had never kept a girlfriend longer than six months, until Kayla. He had slept with more females than he could count on his and your fingers and toes combined. All his life, he had been the man, and nobody fed his ego more than his mother.

Chapter 6

Kayla flew into Dallas International Airport early Saturday morning. She still had not talked to Dareon, despite his persistent calling, and she planned to keep it that way. Kayla had even gone so far as to book a suite at the local downtown Ritz Carlton Hotel, courtesy of Dareon's black AMEX even though she usually stayed in one of the spacious guest rooms at his mother's home. This year, she planned to stay as far away from Dareon as possible, and, personally, she would not have even been there if it was not for Dareon's mother. In the years she had been dating Dareon, Nicole had always been overly warm and caring. And that was the only reason Kayla was even making an appearance at the reunion. *It isn't Nicole's fault that she has a cheating son.*

Casually clad in a pair of destroyed denim Citizen jeans, a pink Lacoste button down covered by an all-black Burberry pea-coat to battle the cold weather, and a pair of cognac colored leather boots that stopped below her knees, Kayla grabbed her signature Louis Vuitton luggage set from the baggage claim and headed to locate a driver from the car company she had hired to drive her to her hotel. After finally spotting the driver carrying a sign bearing her name, she handed him her luggage and was escorted to the awaiting town car. As the driver loaded her bags, Kayla powered on her cell to call her roommates and mother to inform them of her safe arrival. Before long, Kayla was engrossed in conversation with Pharris and Jordan, as the driver cruised through the early morning traffic en route to the Ritz Carlton.

Kayla was just hanging up the phone, when the driver pulled up to her hotel. As soon as she checked in and reached her room, she planned to catch up on her beauty sleep before getting dressed to attend the family reunion. The driver escorted Kayla to the check-in counter, handed her luggage to a bellboy, and then tipped his hat as he departed with the gracious tip Kayla had given. Kayla checked in rapidly, surprised at the swiftness of the transaction, and headed to the escalator. The front desk attendant didn't even ask her for ID; it was like she was expecting her or something. *But, oh, well*, Kayla thought, as she shrugged her shoulders and entered her suite.

As soon as Kayla was out of ear shot, the front desk attendant picked up the phone.

"She's here," she said quickly before hanging up.

Not long after entering the plush suite, Kayla felt an overwhelming need to rest. She stripped out of all her clothing, except her pink lace bra set, and slipped beneath the one thousand thread count sheets to enjoy her slumber. Within minutes, she was sound asleep.

Kayla moaned slightly as she enjoyed the tongue lightly flicking across her nipples and easing down to her belly button. She unknowingly spread her legs as her panties gently slid down her smooth skin and over her freshly manicured feet.

"Mmm..." Kayla moaned as she caught herself trapped between ecstasy and what she thought was a dream.

All of a sudden, her eyes popped open. *Wait a minute!* She was supposed to be in her hotel room. Alone. Kayla snatched off the covers and watched a familiar head lick up and down her thighs as her legs rested on his shoulders. Kayla tried closing her legs while simultaneously pushing Dareon away from doing what he was oh so good at. Her struggling was futile, however, because Dareon expertly found his way to her center, which was betraying her by soaking the sheets. Dareon grabbed Kayla around her hips and sunk his face in deeper. Before Kayla knew it, she had her hands around Dareon's head as she grinded his face and moaned in sweet surrender.

"Can we talk?" Dareon asked Kayla as he emerged from the bathroom after cleaning his face of her juices.

"For what?" Kayla asked irritated that her hormones and lack of sex had allowed her to lose control.

"Because I miss you."

"No, you miss this, Dareon," Kayla said as she derogatorily gestured below to her still unclad bottom. "You're probably gonna want to fuck next."

"I just wanted to taste you. We can fuck later," Dareon said, imitating Lil Wayne as he tickled Kayla.

"Dareon, stop," Kayla said as she giggled and rolled around, trying to bat his fingers away.

Dareon tickled Kayla until she was breathless from laughing and trying to fight him off. Then, he picked her up and carried her to the shower. Dareon removed Kayla's bra before unclothing himself. Then, they got into the shower together. Both enjoyed the massage of the steaming water as they bathed each other in silence and deep thought.

Kayla walked into the bedroom wrapped in one of the hotel's plush towels. She was opening her luggage to pick out an outfit for the reunion when Dareon finally emerged from the bathroom. Kayla had heard his cell phone vibrate on her way out , and judging by the scowl on his face and the constant stroking of his goatee, he was going through something. Instead of asking questions, she continued to carefully select her outfit from the various choices she had brought. As far as she was concerned, Dareon deserved to be stressed for all she had endured being his girlfriend. Kayla finally decided on a pair of Marciano dark denim skinny jeans, a deep red Marciano button-down sweater that was cut deep and enhanced her cleavage, and a pair of red Jimmy Choo stilettos. She removed the towel, ignoring Dareon's watchful gaze, and prepared to get dressed.

When Kayla went into the bathroom to apply her makeup and style her hair, Dareon knelt to the floor and put his head in his hands. *Fuck! Could shit get anymore fucked up?* he thought. Samara had just called him and told him that she planned to keep the baby.

Kayla watched Dareon from the bathroom mirror as she put the finishing touches to her hair. She knew that something was seriously wrong, and her heart tugged at her to go to him. Letting her emotions get the best of her, Kayla walked up behind Dareon and wrapped her arms around him, resting her head on his back.

"Penny for your thoughts," Kayla said, genuinely concerned. Dareon didn't answer; instead, he just pulled her into his arms and held her tight.

****

Dareon and Kayla left the hotel together. Kayla was stunning, as usual, and Dareon matched her fly with a black and red ensemble he'd paired with red and black AirMax. They loaded into Dareon's SUV looking like a power couple and headed towards his childhood home in the hills of North Dallas.

No matter how many times Kayla had been to Dareon's home, the property was always breathtaking. Dareon approached the eighty-five acre property by swiping his access card at the entrance of the sprawling iron gates bearing the family's last name, Anderson, in italicized letters. He, then, approached the circular driveway, already packed with cars, and parked his Escalade. Dareon exited, and then went around to the passenger side to open Kayla's door, so he could escort her into the house.

Kayla had been around Dareon's family before and knew what to expect, but she was not sure how much his mother knew about the recent issues in their relationship. And knowing Ms. Nicole, as soon as she got Kayla alone, she would interrogate her to see if she could find out what Kayla and Dareon had been going through. Personally, Kayla didn't even know if she was ready to deal with questions about Dareon. It was hard to ever discuss their issues without breaking into tears. And this was neither the time nor the place.

Dareon opened the sprawling oak doors for her to enter first, and they walked hand-in-hand through the marble entryway. The reunion was in full swing when they entered. People were laughing loud and playing spades or dominoes, as they waited for the food to get ready. The family usually hosted an inside reunion when the weather was cold, featuring good southern soul food, plenty of liquor, and oldies but goodies that flowed through the sound system.

Kayla and Dareon walked around the spacious home, giving hugs and kisses to the familiar family members, and then separated as Dareon headed to the media room to challenge his rowdy cousins on his PlayStation 3 console. Kayla headed off to find Ms. Nicole, whom she was sure was either in the kitchen with her sisters preparing the food, or out in the back of the house in the gazebo by the lake that had initially convinced Ms. Nicole and her late husband to purchase this sprawling estate.

Kayla, first, tried the kitchen, with no success, and, after greeting Dareon's aunts, she headed out the back door and towards the lake. The backyard of the Anderson residence was a place set for romance novels. The back exit of the home opened up into a sprawling garden maze which led to a bridge over a lake, which included a gazebo. The gazebo was the place where Ms. Nicole usually retreated to clear her mind, or to escape large crowds, especially the rowdy group that usually gathered for the reunion.

Most of her family had escaped the ghetto due to her generosity, but, like the old saying goes, you can take a nigga out the hood, but not the hood out the nigga. It was not unusual for arguments or fights to break out at the reunion, once the family started getting alcohol in their systems.

As Kayla approached the gazebo, shivering against the cold, she noticed the outline of a figure sitting inside, enjoying the view. She picked up her hand to wave, not realizing until she was within feet of the stranger, that it was not Ms. Nicole; and, as a matter of fact, it was not even a female. Seated in the gazebo was one of the finest men Kayla had ever seen.

She could see in his face the relation to Dareon, but that didn't stop her from taking in the appearance of this gorgeous being. Smooth, dark chocolate skin, a muscular build, though not as profound as Dareon. Bedroom eyes, dark wavy hair, and a neatly trimmed goatee had Kayla damn near drooling. There was something about his mannerisms that gave off an edge, and she could tell by the tattoo on his neck, that this family member had not been born with a silver spoon in his mouth.

****

Terry watched the female approaching the gazebo from the corner of his eye. Life in the streets had given him a sixth sense when someone walked up on him unannounced. He could look at her and see she was trouble, because there was no way that a bitch this beautiful could be single. Since he knew she wasn't family, she had to be one of his kinfolk's girls. Terry took in her cappuccino tone, slim fine figure, and her pretty brown eyes. Both of them were caught in a daze as they assessed each other's appearance.

Kayla, slightly embarrassed, finally broke from his intense stare and gave a nervous wave.

"Sorry. I thought you were someone else," she said quickly with a tremble in her voice.

She could not believe she had allowed herself to get so caught up, and especially not with one of Dareon's family members. Regardless of what she and Dareon were going through, she would not be the ho to mess around with a family member. Clearly seeing that Ms. Nicole was nowhere around, Kayla turned around and hauled ass back into the house. She would be damned if someone came outside and caught her out here alone with this guy, whoever he was, because she would hate to have to explain anything to Dareon or Ms. Nicole.

What Kayla did not know, though, was that someone did see the two outside engrossed in each other's stares. Ms. Nicole had been watching from the upstairs master bedroom suite, and she did not like what she saw, not one bit. Ms. Nicole didn't fail to miss the way Terry stared after Kayla as she rushed back into the house.

In her haste to escape the gazebo, Kayla re-entered the house through the back door and ran smack dab into Dareon.

"What's wrong?" he asked as he glanced over her flustered appearance.

"Oh, nothing," Kayla said with a flick of her wrist, perpetuating normalcy. "I just came from trying to find your mom. Have you seen her?"

At that moment, as if on cue, Ms. Nicole descended the winding staircase which led from her master bedroom. She was not a physically attractive woman, which was surprising since Dareon was so gorgeous, but Ms. Nicole maintained a poise of pure elegance, which made even someone as beautiful as Kayla self-conscious. A slender, dark skinned woman, Ms. Nicole had the features of a bird: small beady eyes, a pointy nose, and a slim neck. Aware of her physical appearance, Ms. Nicole clad her small frame with only top designer wear and a multitude of expensive jewelry.

Nicole Carver-Anderson had grown up in a working class family. Her father was a postal worker, and her mother was a cleaning lady. As the eldest of the four Carver daughters, she had been the guardian of her sisters when her parents were working endless overtime hours. She would cook, clean, help with homework, and a vast majority of other chores that should have been reserved only for an adult. Always self-conscious of her appearance, Ms. Nicole would work odd jobs when she had free time, and combine that with money she received from her parents to support her obsession with clothing and beauty products.

Always a straight-A student despite her full schedule, Ms. Nicole received a scholarship to Harvard after high school graduation, which was where she met Dareon's father. They both graduated at the top of their classes. Instead of utilizing her business degree, Ms. Nicole helped Dareon's father establish his law firm and spent her leisure time managing her household. The only thing that Ms. Nicole longed for was a baby, and it was not until many fertility treatments later that she became pregnant with her miracle child, Dareon.

Ms. Nicole looked like the epitome of class for the reunion, knowingly overdressed compared to the clothing of the other family members. Whereas the majority of the guests had on jeans, Ms. Nicole looked immaculate in a beige designer suit, a pair of gold Jimmy Choo stilettos, and pearls accented with diamonds. She always knew how to make everyone else feel as if they were the ones who were out of place, even though she was the one grossly overdressed.

As she approached the landing, Dareon swept her into his arms. Ms. Nicole gave her only child a peck on the cheek, and then gently broke from his hug. She, then, gave Kayla a quick hug, and ushered her son's girlfriend into the kitchen to help her prepare the dining table for dinner. Unlike most black families, Ms. Nicole was not one to have the family waiting all day for dinner.

"I just came from the gazebo trying to find you," Kayla told Ms. Nicole as she followed her into the kitchen.

"Oh, well, I was upstairs getting freshened up for dinner," Ms. Nicole replied. "I thought I saw you through my bedroom window. Did you get a chance to meet my nephew while you were out there, dear?" Ms. Nicole asked nonchalantly as she slyly monitored Kayla's reaction.

Nephew....Kayla thought as she pictured the LL Cool J lips and bedroom eyes attached to the face she had admired in the gazebo.

"I-I think s-so," Kayla stammered, confirming Ms. Nicole's suspicions.

Ms. Nicole was not a fool, and she knew, from the feeling in her gut and the stammer in Kayla's voice, that she would have to nip this situation in the bud immediately. She would be damned if her son was made a fool of by this middle class bitch and her ghetto-ass nephew. Ms. Nicole knew better than anyone that, after all Kayla had been through with Dareon, she was probably looking for someone to help mend her broken heart, but it would not be Terry.

Kayla helped bring the food into the dining area, as the family gathered around the massive oak dining table to pray. Dareon's uncle, Percy, a backwoods preacher from Mississippi, led the family in a drawn out twenty-minute prayer, thanking God for everything, including the paint chips on the walls. After a chorus of 'Amens', the family was finally able to dig into the many casseroles of greens, sweet potatoes, mashed potatoes, fried chicken, fried fish, pork chops, macaroni and cheese, cornbread, and vast arrays of fruits, pies, and cobblers. Before long, the spacious home was filled with laughter and the sounds of silverware clanking against china.

After everyone had eaten to their capacity, it was time for music and dancing. As Kayla did the bus stop to "Before I Let Go", she failed to notice Terry staring at her from across the room. *Damn! She is fine,* he thought as he licked his lips.

"Stop staring at my girl, playboy," Dareon said as he walked up behind Terry and playfully gave him a shove.

"Oh, that's you, lil cuz?" Terry said, faking amazement.

He had heard that Dareon's girl was a dime from other family members, but damn. And to think, Dareon's dumb ass had some broad knocked up, from what he had heard through the family gossip network.

Dareon and Terry chilled for a few minutes, catching up on old times. While Dareon had been making headlines across ESPN, Terry had been in Houston, making his money in the streets, the only way he knew how. Similar to Dareon, though, Terry drove a fire-ass whip, a customized, fully-loaded pearl white Denali, sitting on twenty-six inch diamond encrusted blades. But unlike Dareon, Terry's whip had not been purchased by his mother.

Terrence Jaylen Carver was the son of Dareon's mother's youngest sister, Priscilla. Priscilla had given Terry everything she could during his childhood, which usually did not amount to much, considering her meager earnings as an elementary school cafeteria worker. Terry had begun selling weed at the age of thirteen to help his mother out on bills, eluding her by telling her that the extra cash showing up around the house came from a paper route. At sixteen, Terry had upgraded to cocaine, and now, at the age of twenty-three, he was a major D-Boy, known for having the best white girl in the city of Houston.

"Kayla, come and meet my cousin," Dareon called out to Kayla as the song came to an end.

Hesitantly, Kayla put on her best calm-and-collected face and walked over to meet Terry. For some reason, she felt like he took her out of her element. Usually able to keep her composure when she felt it was required, Kayla felt like her knees would turn into liquid when she came within feet of him. *Why have I never seen him before?* Kayla wondered as she stuck out her hand to greet Dareon's cousin. The exchange was brief, the shaking of hands accompanied by a short "Hello", but both of them felt the bolts of electricity the instant their skin touched. This could be nothing but trouble, and they both felt, without even having to communicate, that the best thing to do would be to get through this weekend, with as little interaction as possible.

Chapter 7

Dareon, why in the fuck have you not been answering your damn phone? You act like I am not carrying your child," a pissed off Samara screamed into the phone.

Dareon was lying on his sofa with the phone pulled away from his ear, watching *SportsCenter* on ESPN. He'd had just about enough of Samara's ass and all the drama she was causing behind her baby. Shit! He had told her ass over and over again to have an abortion, and his mom had even offered her $20,000, but Samara was relentless. She was determined to bear an Anderson because she knew that, in the long run, Dareon's seed would be worth millions. As soon as Dareon hung up on Samara for about the fifth time that day and powered his phone off, Kayla entered the apartment with her key.

Dareon had given Kayla a key to his apartment after they came back from Dallas in an effort to regain her trust. He knew he had fucked up big by impregnating Samara, and now that Samara was intent on letting the world know she was keeping the baby, he was pulling out everything he had to save his relationship. Giving Kayla a key to the apartment did not necessarily guarantee Dareon's faithfulness, though. He was just utilizing the hotels and motels around Baton Rouge more frequently. And now, when he fucked another female besides Kayla, he would double up on the protection, because Dareon would be damned if another bitch trapped him like Samara had.

Kayla plopped down on the sofa under Dareon and gave him a peck on the cheek. Ever since she had gotten the key to his condo, she felt like their relationship was getting stronger. Dareon could no longer hide a bitch behind his double-bolted door, and, as far as she knew, he was, at least, trying to be faithful. Despite the rumors of Dareon being seen with other females around Baton Rouge, Kayla had decided that she was going to let go and let God, if Dareon was cheating again, the truth would come to light, and, next time, she was going to leave his ass for good. Dareon wrapped his arms around her and kissed her on the neck. He did love Kayla, but, right now, he didn't want monogamy. Kayla was wifey material. He knew that, but—damn!—as of right now, the last thing on Dareon's mind was marriage.

Dareon and Kayla lay on the couch for about an hour, before finally getting up and heading to the bedroom. Kayla had spent most of the night at her apartment studying, and she had decided last minute to go by Dareon's condo to sleep. She had been spending just about every night by Dareon's place anyway and didn't see why tonight should be an exception. In the back of her head, she knew that, as long as she spent the night with Dareon, he could not spend the night with anyone else. Even though she was choosing to believe that Dareon was being faithful, she knew that if she gave this nigga an inch, he would take five miles.

Bzzz. Bzzz.

Kayla awoke to the relentless vibrating of Dareon's phone. Pissed that her sleep had been broken, Kayla reached over Dareon, who was obviously in a deep sleep, and snatched up the phone. As soon as she said hello though, the caller, who was so eager to speak with Dareon, hung up. Kayla unhooked Dareon's phone from the charger and took it into the living room, after silently closing Dareon's bedroom door behind her. This bitch who had hung up the phone in her damn face was about to get cussed out, and she knew that, if Dareon woke up, he would just take his phone and power it off. Kayla sat on the couch and dialed the unsaved number back.

"Is there a reason why you calling phones and hanging up, bitch?" Kayla asked as soon as the female on the other end answered.

Hearing Kayla's voice, the female again disconnected. Frustrated, Kayla returned Dareon's phone to the charger, before reassuming her place in the bed. After a few minutes of tossing and turning, Kayla was finally able to force herself back to sleep.

****

The next morning Kayla debated asking Dareon who the mystery caller was, but finally decided to leave it alone, knowing that without valid proof, Dareon would just disregard the whole incident. Kayla knew she was playing the fool, but, instead of facing reality, she just told herself that she was doing the right thing by not escalating an issue that may really be nothing.

Since morning classes had been cancelled that day due to a mandatory seminar, which no one chose to attend, Kayla and Dareon decided to go to the Waffle House for breakfast, once they finally rolled out of bed. Kayla and Dareon took a quick shower together, and then both got dressed for the day since they would not be returning to Dareon's place due to afternoon classes. Kayla looked like a walking advertisement, as usual, when they left the condo.

All during her afternoon class, Kayla could not concentrate as she repeatedly replayed in her mind the incident from the night before. No matter how she tried to downplay it, she could not. Each and every scenario she presented to herself to try and deceive her common sense, came back to the same conclusion: the only reason a ho would be blowing up a nigga like Dareon's phone at three A.M. was for some dick. By the end of class, Kayla had decided that she was going to find out the identity of this mystery caller, and either confirm or negate her suspicions about her so-called boyfriend.

As a truly scorned woman, as soon as Kayla got into her car after class, she dialed the number from the night before by memory. Any woman who has ever been cheated on can tell you that the experience blesses you with a memory like an elephant, especially when it comes to names, addresses, and phone numbers.

A female voice answered on the first ring. This time around, though, Kayla tried to take the conversation in a different direction. Instead of utilizing her usual pissed off tone when it came to bullshit situations like this, she decided she was going to kill this chick with kindness.

"Hello, this is Kayla, Dareon's girlfriend, and I was wondering if you could tell me the reason you found it necessary to blow up his phone this morning?" Kayla asked in her sweetest tone.

Clearly with more balls than the night before, the female on the other end replied, "How about you call and ask your so-called man since he's on his way over here?"

Kayla slammed the phone down and sped the half mile to Dareon's condo. Just as she was about to turn left onto his street, she saw his Escalade exiting his building. Instead of confronting him right there and then and fucking him up on sight like she had it on her mind to do, Kayla eased her Benz onto a side street, so she could inconspicuously follow behind him. In a few minutes, Kayla felt it in her gut that she was about to find out whether her man was back to his old tricks.

Kayla followed Dareon as he passed through the LSU campus and headed toward the interstate. She made sure to stay, at least, two to three cars behind him, and, for once, she was glad that her car was inconspicuous. There had to be hundreds of silver Mercedes around the city. Dareon eased his Escalade onto I-10 and then I-12, all while Kayla followed behind him like a woman on a mission.

"Girl, where is his ass at now?" an excited Pharris asked Kayla.

Kayla had called both Jordan and Pharris on three-way within a few seconds of making the decision to follow Dareon.

"He's exiting on Sherwood Forest," Kayla replied.

It was like she could feel her heart in the pit of her stomach as she struggled to breathe, because it was now official, none of Dareon's niggas stayed on this side of Baton Rouge.

"Girl, I hope you kick his ass if he is by some ho's house and hers, too," Jordan said all too calmly.

"Gotta go. He's turning into an apartment complex," Kayla responded quickly as she disconnected the call.

Kayla watched Dareon park his truck and walk up a flight of stairs to an apartment. She, then, watched as a very curvy female answered the door and escorted Dareon in. Fuming mad, Kayla dialed her roommates back.

"It's fuckin' official. I just watched this nigga go inside of some bitch's house. What should I do now?" Kayla asked, more to herself than to her roommates.

"Girl, we are on our way. Just sit there and make sure no one sees you," Jordan said.

****

In record time, Jordan and Pharris pulled up to the apartment complex where Kayla had seen Dareon enter this other female's home. They followed Kayla's directions to the other end of the apartment complex where she had parked to conceal her car, but where she could still see Dareon's truck and the female's apartment. Jordan and Pharris stepped out of the car looking like they were ready for battle. Both girls had on black Victoria's Secret Pink collection sweats and matching hoodies with the latest all black Jordans. They had even brought an identical set of sweats and Jordans for Kayla to change into. Kayla did not yet know what Jordan and Pharris had planned, but as she changed into her battle gear in the back of Jordan's Porsche Cayenne SUV, she knew that, in the words of Young Joc, it was going down.

As soon as Kayla was dressed, Jordan pulled a sack of goodies out of the back of her SUV. Inside the bag were three baseball bats, two cans of white spray paint, and a pocket knife. *This bitch is crazy, too,* Kayla thought as all three girls pulled their hoodies over their heads and got into war mode. They all knew what time it was. No words were needed.

Glad that the sun was going down and that the apartment complex was in a secluded area with minimal traffic, the girls walked over to Dareon's Escalade with their goodies clutched close. Jordan began the assault by stooping down and slitting one of Dareon's rear tires. Kayla and Pharris followed her lead by spray painting obscenities all over the truck. As crazy as Kayla thought she was, she could not have pulled this one off without her girls. Once the body of the truck was completely destroyed, the girls got out their baseball bats and all took one swing, shattering his front and back windshields and his driver's side window. Then, they ran back to their vehicles and burned out. Thank God for the small things, not one car approached nor did one neighbor appear, while they were vandalizing Dareon's prized possession.

On the way back to their house, Kayla and the girls stopped by a dumpster and threw out the evidence. There was no way that this crime could be traced back to them. All the girls had too much riding on their reputations to get into trouble behind a situation like this. But honestly, as far as they were all concerned, Dareon deserved the shit. It was just too bad a court wouldn't see it that way.

When the girls got home, they all hit the showers, and threw their sweats in the washing machine. Once everyone was showered, and their sweats were dried and put away, the girls retreated to the living room, erupting into a chorus of laughter as they pictured the expression on Dareon's face when he saw his truck. Just then, a loud clap of thunder, followed by a downpour erupted outside, causing the girls to laugh even harder. If Dareon thought he was mad, the rain was going to piss him off even more 'cause there was not a body shop in Baton Rouge that would be able to get to his car until the morning at the earliest, no matter how much money he had.

****

Knock! Knock! Bang! Bang!

Kayla woke to the noise of what sounded like someone trying to break down her front door.

"Kayla! It's Dareon," she heard one of her roommates whisper from the darkness.

Kayla glanced at her clock, it was two A.M. *Why couldn't this shit wait until the morning?* Kayla rolled out of bed and threw on her robe. Not knowing what to expect from Dareon, she, also, picked up her keys that held a can of mace, just in case this nigga got to trippin'. It was too late for all that bullshit. If he wouldn't have been by that bitch's house, his car wouldn't have got fucked up. Kayla shooed her roommates back to their rooms, advising them that, if they heard any indication that sounded like she needed help, they had better come running.

"What the fuck do you want, Dareon?" Kayla asked as she pulled open the door with the security latch still in place. She could only see a sliver of his face, but she could tell that he was pissed.

"I know you fucked up my truck, Kayla. What the fuck is wrong with you?" he snapped at her.

"That's what's wrong with niggas now. Y'all know too fuckin' much," Kayla replied. "Just like you should have known your dumb ass was going to get caught."

"Come outside, Kayla," Dareon said as he tried to push his way inside the apartment.

"No, bitch," Kayla replied calmly. "And I suggest you get the fuck off my property before I call the police," Kayla said as she slammed the door in his face.

Pissed off, but unsure of whether Kayla was bluffing about calling the police, Dareon hopped back into his rented Explorer and headed back toward Sherwood Forest. As he returned to the same location where his car had been vandalized and the girl it had been vandalized over, Dareon raved and ranted about how he planned to fuck Kayla up. The only thing stopping him was her threat to call the police, and the fact that he didn't know just what she was truly capable of.

Chapter 8

Kayla slept well that night. As a matter of fact, she couldn't remember a time she had slept better. Just knowing that she had fazed Dareon by fucking up his truck gave her a sick sense of satisfaction. And also adding to her satisfaction was the fact that she and her girls had decided, after Dareon left the night before, to take a weekend getaway to South Padre Island. It was just what they all needed to clear their minds. They wanted to chill until things cooled down in Baton Rouge. Their plane would be leaving at noon that day, so Kayla went to wake up her roommates, so they all could pack and be at the airport in New Orleans on time.

The girls loaded into Jordan's SUV, since they had all packed like they would not be returning, and headed to the airport around nine A.M. Kayla had decided to leave her cell behind, and had informed only her mother where she would be going and how to contact her in case of any emergency because the only other two people who she talked to on a regular basis were going to Padre with her.

****

The weather was nippy, so the girls were disappointed they wouldn't be enjoying the beach in swimsuits, but, oh well, there was always still Dirty Al's. Every time the girls went to South Padre, they ate at Dirty Al's, which was one of the best seafood restaurants in the United States, and housed the freshest seafood and delicious daiquiris made with wine.

Their plane landed in Brownsville, the nearest airport to South Padre, at approximately two P.M., and the girls went straight to Enterprise to rent a car to drive to South Padre. Usually a car was not needed to get around South Padre, but, since it was technically still winter, the girls knew walking would be completely unreasonable. They rented a Dodge Nitro and drove the short distance to South Padre to check into their hotel and to change clothes to go eat lunch.

After checking into the hotel, the girls each took turns showering and getting dressed. Even though the ladies were dressed down, compared to their usual garb, their designer jeans and low cut tops were sure to turn heads in the laidback, beach town. The trio left the La Copa Resort looking like divas, and drove down the main street in South Padre to Dirty Al's, laughing and joking all the way. It felt good to be away from school and drama, even if only for a weekend.

The girls arrived at Dirty Al's and directed themselves to a table. They already knew what they wanted to order, so there was no need to look at a menu. They would be splitting a Dirty Al's seafood platter which came with enough fish, shrimp, and French fries to feed a small army. As soon as the waitress came, the girls placed their order, and had the waitress immediately bring them daiquiris. This was their getaway, and there was nothing wrong with starting it off with alcohol before sunset.

"Girl, do you see those guys back there in that corner?" Jordan said, signaling with her eyes towards a table near the back. Simultaneously, Kayla and Pharris turned slightly, just enough to see the fine specimens that Jordan was referring to. Almost instantly, Kayla let out a short gasp.

"The one in the red shirt is Dareon's cousin. The one I was telling y'all about," Kayla said.

"What is he doing here?" both Pharris and Jordan asked in unison.

"But he is fine as hell," Pharris said, laughing.

Terry had noticed Kayla the second she walked through the door. The bitch was bad, and so were her female companions. He was in South Padre to handle a business deal with a new connect from Mexico, but there was not a valid reason he could think of why Kayla should be in South Padre in the middle of the school semester. Terry licked his lips as he watched Kayla suck on the straw of the daiquiri the waitress placed in front of her. As Terry watched Kayla, a petite brown-skinned girl walked over to the table shared by his two partners-in-crime. Terry recognized her as one of the girls Kayla had entered the restaurant with a few minutes earlier.

"Hi. I'm Jordan," she said, staring directly at Terry's boy, Chris. "And I was wondering if me and my girls could join you?"

"It's whatever," Chris said, making room for Jordan.

Chris was just Jordan's type: tall, light-skinned, and built like a basketball player with a smooth baby face and a dimple in each cheek. As a matter of fact, as she scooted unnecessarily close to Chris, Jordan noticed that all three of the dudes were fine as hell. Shon, the other figure in Terry's crew, looked so similar to Morris Chestnut that he was often mistaken for him. The only difference was that he was slightly less muscular, and a little taller. When Pharris saw Shon after Jordan waived her and Kayla over, her heart almost skipped a beat. Pharris quickly snatched the seat next to Shon before Kayla tried to steal it, and flashed him a million dollar smile which showed off her pearly whites.

Kayla was the only one reluctant to join the table. She could still recall vividly how Terry made her feel at the reunion, and she didn't feel that she could keep her composure if he got too close to her. Finally making it to the table, Kayla took the only available seat next to Terry, and tried her best to look casual. Jordan and Pharris were already engaged in conversations with their new beaus, and she and Terry sat in silence.

"So, Kayla, what brings you to Padre?" Terry asked, trying to break the ice. He could sense that Kayla was uncomfortable.

"Just a quick getaway," Kayla answered and said a silent prayer that Terry and Dareon were not close enough to where Terry would discuss her whereabouts. She did not want Dareon knowing where she was and preferred that he think she was in Baton Rouge and just ignoring his ass.

"So, you just decided to come down here out the blue, even though I know school is still in for the semester…I think, maybe, you are in some shit." He stared at Kayla like a chastising parent.

"Maybe, that's the story of your life," Kayla answered, glaring back like a defiant child.

"Maybe, you are right."

Kayla could tell he was taunting her.

"Well, don't make your problems mine," Kayla said, leaning close enough into Terry that she could smell his spearmint breath.

"The food is here," chorused Pharris and a bubbly Jordan.

Kayla was thankful for the reprieve from the flirtatious conversation. Jerking away from Terry's gaze, Kayla focused her attention on the large platter of food. Clearly, the chemistry Kayla felt for Terry was mutual, and that was the last thing that either of them needed.

The newfound friends sat, ate, and joked with each other the entire meal. After all plates had been scraped bare, the men took care of the bill and escorted the ladies to their rented vehicle. Numbers were exchanged, and promises were made for the trios to meet later that night.

The group decided to go out to the Sky Bar, a small club popular among the locals. The three girls clad in Michael Kors from head to toe met up with Terry and his friends in front of their resort. Their dates looked almost as good in their Ed Hardy fits and fresh white on white Air Forces that looked straight out the box. Chris drove the group to the club in his white Navigator that sat on twenty-six inch rims. When they pulled up in front of the club, Chris turned his keys over to the valet service, and each man escorted his female for the night into the dimly lit nightclub. After a few shots of Patrón, the whole crew was having fun, dancing the night away as time flew by.

The group didn't leave the club until it closed, and by that time, the females were thoroughly wasted. This was their getaway trip, and no expense was spared in their quest to have fun. In the words of a very drunk Jordan: "You only live once". Since Jordan and Pharris had made plans with Chris and Shon, Terry asked that he and Kayla be dropped off on the beach behind the resort where she was staying. A walk on the beach seemed their most sensible option, since a rendezvous in the hotel was out of the question.

The breeze near the beach was cold, so Terry purchased a blanket from a vendor on the beach to wrap around Kayla's shoulders.

"So, you ready to talk about why you are here?" Terry asked Kayla as they walked barefoot in the sand.

"Because all men are dogs," Kayla said in a barely audible whisper.

"No," Terry said as he turned her around to face him and made her stare into his eyes. "All boys are dogs. And people can only do what you allow them to do to you."

Terry wrapped his arms around Kayla as he stared into her face. He could see all the hurt and pain that her eyes held with just with one long glance. For some reason, he felt like he needed to protect her. He had learned his lesson a long time ago about how cruel life could be when you were in love with someone who had a love greater than you. Terry cringed at the memory of his past and closed his eyes to erase it.

"I see that I am not the only one who's been hurt," Kayla said as she rested her head on his chest.

Almost automatically, Terry wrapped her in his arms. As far as he was concerned, the conversation about him was done. He had closed the heartbreak chapter in his life a long time ago, and tonight was not the night to reopen it.

"Terry."

"Hmmm."

"I think I need to…"

At that moment, Kayla pulled herself from his arms and ran over to a patch of grass. *Please don't throw up. Please don't throw up,* she repeated over and over in her head. Clearly, they had gone too hard that night, and she refused to make a fool of herself in front of Dareon's cousin. Terry chuckled at Kayla's bent over form kneeling in the grass, as he went over to rub her back. It was time to get her back to her hotel room. He watched her back constrict and turned his head as the contents of her stomach were spilled onto the cool South Padre Beach.

"I'm so embarrassed," Kayla whispered before breaking into tears.

She was absolutely mortified, and all that she wanted to do was bury her head in the sand. Terry lifted Kayla into his arms like a baby and carried her to the resort where she was staying. He knew that she was not in any shape to get back to her room alone. As he carried her to the elevator, Kayla retrieved her room key from her purse and, in between bouts of tears, directed him to the correct suite. He actually found the situation comical.

Once inside the hotel suite, Terry laid Kayla on the bed and went to run her a bath in the oversized marble garden tub. Once the tub had reached near capacity, Terry undressed Kayla and placed her inside. It was the least he could do for contributing to her inebriated state.

"Do you need anything else?" he asked as he shut the door to allow her privacy.

"Just for you to be here when I get out," Kayla said, before leaning back to enjoy the suds as they covered her tired body.

After a few minutes, Terry went back into the bathroom to check on Kayla. When he saw she had fallen asleep, he gently bathed her and then wrapped one of the oversized hotel towels around her and lifted her from the tub. As he carried her to her bed, she rested her head against his shoulder and continued her peaceful slumber. He couldn't decide which bag was hers, so he left her wrapped in the towel and tucked her in. Just as he was preparing to leave the room, Kayla reached out and grabbed his arm.

"Can you just stay until I fall asleep?" she asked, semi-delirious.

Terry knew that the right thing to do would be to turn and leave. But he didn't. Instead, he allowed the towel to be their barrier and crawled into bed next to her. Clearly aroused by the naked body pressed against him, Terry wrapped his arms around her and kissed her forehead before willing himself to sleep.

Kayla awoke early the next morning and rolled over to find the space next to her empty. Immediately, she popped up and wondered, *Where is Terry?* Even though she had spent most of the night intoxicated, she could still remember feeling Terry's strong arms around her. Pissed that she did not have her cell phone, Kayla picked herself up out of bed and went to take a cold shower. Hopefully, the shower would wash some sense into her because she knew that she should not be missing the presence of Dareon's first cousin.

****

Terry sat on the beach facing the water. *What the fuck happened last night?* Terry could not deny the attraction that he felt for Kayla, even after watching her vomit on the beach. It had taken everything in him to pull himself from the bed once Kayla fell asleep. From the first moment he had laid eyes on Kayla, he had been mesmerized by everything about her. He wanted to be her protector, to shield her from any more pain. Watching Kayla was like watching an Oscar performance because he knew that, behind her smile, her spirit had been broken and was in need of repair.

"So, how was your night, bitch?" Jordan asked Kayla as she came bouncing into the hotel suite.

"Memorable." She was still slightly horrified about throwing up on the beach. "Let's just say no more Patrón for me anytime soon. And where the hell is Pharris?"

"Well, if Pharris had a night like me, she's probably still trying to limp her ass back here," Jordan said, laughing.

"I know you didn't fuck that nigga, Jordan?"

"Who me?" Jordan asked, placing her hand over her heart and pretending to faint.

Kayla rolled her eyes, but could not help laughing at her obnoxious friend. One thing about Jordan, she lived life to the fullest. As Jordan laid across Kayla's bed, entertaining her with stories from her sex-filled night, Pharris walked in, looking like she'd had anything but a good time.

"Ask me why this nigga couldn't even eat pussy right?" she said as she made room for herself on Kayla's bed right smack in the middle of her two roommates. "And then he had the nerve to think he was going to get some."

"Well, sorry you bitches had such a pathetic night," Jordan smirked.

At that comment, Pharris threw a pillow at Jordan, and, before the girls knew it, they were embroiled in a full blown pillow fight. The girls chilled in the room till around noon, opting to order room service instead of going out for breakfast. Unsure of what the day would hold, they decided to start it off with a full service spa they had seen near the beach. After each girl had received a facial, mud bath, and full body massages, they went to the beach to plan the remainder of their activities.

****

Terry, Chris, and Shon decided to go and chill on the beach after wrapping up their business deal. None of them had really talked about the night before because they had all gotten together at the last minute to meet with their new connect. The crew had heard good things about an up and coming mover and shaker in Mexico with competitive prices and couldn't resist negotiating a deal. But now, as they chilled on the beach, they could reminisce on their dates.

"So, what's up with you and Dareon's girl?" Chris asked Terry in all seriousness, reminding him that he was dealing with a precious situation.

"Not shit," Terry said, unsure of whom he was trying to convince, himself or his boys.

"Well, shit! Her friend Jordan is a fool," Chris said, steering the topic away from Terry and Kayla.

"Well, her friend Pharris was trippin'. She was trying to make a nigga work too hard for the pussy," Shon added, shaking his head. "The bitch is bad, but damn, man, I got a wife at home. The last thing I need to be is stressing over some ass."

As Shon and Chris talked about the night before, Terry's mind again drifted back to Kayla. The hardest thing he had to do last night was keep his hands to himself, but, whenever he did get inside of her, it would be when she was sober and knew he was what she wanted. Terry ran his fingers over the tattoo on his neck...*Samantha*...and snapped back into reality. *What the hell am I thinking? Kayla is off limits.*

Kayla recognized the three figures walking towards them before either of her roommates did.

"How are you, ladies?" Chris said, looking at Jordan.

Jordan eyed Chris seductively before saying in unison with Kayla and Pharris, "Fine."

Kayla looked at Terry, trying to capture his averting eyes. *What's up with him?* She wondered as she half listened to her roommates chatting with Shon and Chris.

"You don't talk much, do you?" Pharris asked Terry as she stared from him to Kayla.

"Depends on the situation," he replied.

Pharris waved him off and jumped back into the conversation with Shon, Chris, and Jordan. Shon may not have been the ideal fuck buddy, but, at least, he was entertaining.

As if by impulse, Kayla grabbed Terry's hand and pulled him away from the group. Not usually this aggressive with someone who was practically a stranger,

Kayla surprised even herself as she continued to hold his hand after they had departed from the group. They walked down the beach in silence before Kayla finally broke the ice.

"I'm really sorry about last night."

Terry laughed. "Yeah, but I had already figured you were a lightweight."

"Kiss my ass."

"Bend over."

Kayla couldn't help but to laugh at the racy thought that ran through her head. She could think of a handful of places she wanted him to kiss in conjunction with her ass.

"What's so funny?"

"You don't even want to know."

"You're going to tell me." And with that Terry, released Kayla's hand and flipped her over his shoulder.

"What are you doing?" Kayla yelled out in panic. She could tell that Terry was heading towards the cold Gulf waters.

"So, what were you laughing about?" he asked as he held her in place over his shoulder with one hand and removed his shoes and socks with the other.

"Nothing. I promise."

"Not a good answer."

By that point, Terry was within feet of the water. Kayla trembled at the thought of being dunked in the frigid waves. She squirmed and beat Terry's shoulders, but he was relentless.

"Kayla, you have about ten seconds before you can kiss your clothes goodbye."

"But, I can't tell you."

Kayla could feel her cheeks turning a blustering red, and she tried to think of a lie to cover her ass. There was no way she could tell him about the pornographic thoughts that she had racing through her head. *First the vomiting, and now this? Can I embarrass myself anymore in front of this man?*

"Three seconds, Kayla."

Fuck it. Kayla crossed her arms and prepared to meet the freezing Gulf waters. There was not a way in hell she was going to tell Terry anything.

"I'm not telling you anything."

And with that, Kayla closed her eyes and prepared for the worst. But miraculously, she felt Terry come to a complete stop.

"That bad, huh?"

Kayla opened her eyes and cocked her head in his direction. *Was he just bluffing the whole time?*

"That bad," she replied, erupting into laughter.

"Too bad."

At that moment Terry rushed towards the water, just as a large wave was washing across the shore. Kayla barely had time to close her mouth before her body was drenched in the frosty South Padre water.

"Son of a bi—"

The last of her sentence was drowned out by another wave hitting their bodies. Kayla could hear the laughs of their friends coming from the beach. She was literally chilled to the bone and could feel her temperature rising. Her clothes, her shoes, her hair, and her body were completely soaked.

"Take me to my damn room!" she screamed out at Terry. He was also soaked, and she couldn't believe that he didn't even look fazed by the frigid cold.

He could hear the irritation in her voice and found it amusing. She should have told him what he asked, and they would not have been in this situation. Instead of waiting for the next wave though, he packed Kayla like a sack of wet potatoes back to the shore.

"I could kill you," Kayla whispered between her clenched, chattering teeth.

Instead of answering back, Terry waved to their audience on the beach and headed to Kayla's resort for the second time that weekend. *She'll get over it.* He thought about letting her off his shoulder, but he knew that her inability to control the situation was driving her crazy. So hold her on his shoulder he did, until they reached the door of the hotel suite.

"Let's hope my key still works, asshole." Kayla glared at him as she removed the room key from the back pocket of her soaking wet jeans.

She was slightly disappointed when the lights on the door illuminated green and when she heard the click of the locks unlatching. Now, she couldn't prove her point.

Before entering the room, she turned around to glare at her perpetrator.

"I should make you go back to wherever you came from," she said, looking him up and down.

He was also soaked, and she almost smirked when she saw him shiver slightly. Satisfied that he was also suffering, she led the way into the room. Throwing Terry a towel, she began to remove her saturated clothing. Kayla could feel Terry's eyes on her body and couldn't help but to make the most out of the strip tease. She made sure to bend over just right as she gathered their clothing to place in a bag for emergency one hour dry-cleaning.

Terry tried to keep his eyes off of Kayla's body, but he couldn't seem to peel them away. For the life of him, he could not understand the rationale behind her changing in his presence. The physical attraction was obvious, and the sight of Kayla in her black lace panties and matching bra were doing wonders on his libido.

"Are you going to finish getting undressed?"

Kayla seductively looked Terry up and down. Her anger had dissipated, and she was more than aroused at his shirtless physique. At that moment, she could have cared less about Dareon. She was on vacation and deserved the opportunity to have some fun. *So what that Terry was Dareon's cousin?* Dareon was deserving of the same regard that he had shown her throughout the course of their relationship, and she didn't see the point in fantasizing about someone two feet away from her.

Terry knew that all kinds of lines were about to be crossed, but his judgment was too clouded to stop the inevitable. His other head had already taken control. He didn't stop Kayla from tracing kisses from his collarbone up to his lips.

He lifted her in the air as their tongues danced in each other's mouth, and she wrapped her legs around his waist. As he carried her to the bed, he unhooked her bra with his spare hand and let his tongue explore the sensitive places on her neck. It didn't take long for everything to unfold, and the ripping of a signature gold package signified the means to the end. All rationale went out the window, and Dareon did not cross either of their minds.

It only took seconds for Kayla and Terry to find their rhythm. Terry rotated his pelvis against Kayla as he went fast then slow and then fast again. Kayla wrapped her legs around Terry and dug her nails into his back, as she tried to drown out her moans by burying her head in his chest. Not satisfied until he made her scream, Terry stroked Kayla faster and harder, until finally she was screaming out his name along with unintelligible gibberish. When he felt her leg begin to tremble, he increased his pace.

"I'm cumming!" Kayla finally screamed out as she clenched her vaginal muscles around his dick. And with that, he also came in what felt like torrents. The guilt came only minutes after the passion.

"What the fuck did we just do?" Terry wondered aloud, looking down at Kayla's naked body sprawled underneath his own naked form. Kayla was silent for a few seconds and tried to process her feelings about the situation. Unlike Terry, it was not guilt that plagued her mind, but the thought that their tryst would end in South Padre. Dareon had made his bed, and she deserved to be able to relish in this moment.

"We did what we wanted to do," she finally replied, planting kisses on his neck.

"Kayla, listen. I am not about to be your rebound nigga."

Even though it took a massive amount of will power, Terry pulled away from her lips and tried to talk some reason into his cousin's girlfriend.

"We need to just forget that this shit ever happened."

"Why should we have to forget?" Kayla could not believe the audacity of this nigga.

"Because I am not about to be the rebound that you use because of your shit with Dareon."

"So, that's what you think this is, Terry?" Kayla asked pointedly. Before he could answer, she continued, "Since the first time I met you, I have felt this almost magnetic attraction to you. I know that you felt it, too. It showed in your eyes, the same way it showed in mine, all the way back in Dallas. So don't you dare come at me like this is just some random-ass mistake? And so fuckin' what if you are Dareon's cousin? One man's trash is another man's treasure, and your treasure just happened to come down from the same bloodline."

Tears streamed down Kayla's face. She had no idea where this emotion was coming from, but she knew everything that she was saying was true. Once again, she was unhappy because of Dareon.

"It's not that simple, Kayla. You are talking about my family. And I wouldn't want Dareon or any other family member moving in on my girl. Real talk. A nigga who wasn't family would get his ass murdered for the same shit. And on top of that, Kayla, you don't know my life—"

"But I don't care," Kayla interrupted as she pouted, poking out her bottom lip.

Terry did his best to dry her tears with his fingers. He didn't enjoy being in the company of any crying woman, especially when he was contributing to her tears. And on top of that, the sight of Kayla's naked form was starting to bring his other head back to life.

"Kayla, this situation is fucked up. Let's just take a step back and..."

His words were interrupted by Kayla's lips pressing against his own. Terry leaned in and gently sucked on Kayla's bottom lip. Kayla moaned as his tongue found its way inside of her mouth. Abruptly ending the kiss, Terry began to lightly kiss and nibble on Kayla's neck and earlobes. Kayla again moaned. *How does he know all of my secret spots?* Their intense kisses were interrupted by an abrupt knock on the door.

"Dry cleaning!" A voice yelled out from the opposite side of the door.

That was just the distraction that Terry needed to tear himself from the situation. He sauntered to the door naked and took the bag from the shocked attendant. Kayla couldn't help but to prop on her elbows and watch the show from the bed. That was definitely one thing that Dareon and Terry had in common, such big egos.

"Come on, Kayla. Get dressed. Let's go back out to the beach before we make this situation more fucked up than it already is."

Chapter 9

When Terry had called to let Shon and Chris know that he was headed back to the beach with Kayla, he was told to meet them back at Dirty Al's. When Kayla and Terry walked in together, everyone at the table turned to stare.

"So, what did we miss?" Jordan asked as she stared at Kayla.

Kayla ignored her and sat down. The tension between her and Terry was thick enough to cut with a knife. They had not said much to each other on the walk back to meet up with the crew, and she couldn't get rid of the foreboding feeling that told her their dealings were over. Jordan and Pharris glanced at each other, and then at Kayla, but kept their comments to themselves.

Terry entered the restaurant after Kayla and took the seat next to her. He didn't want their situation to appear awkward, but he felt her flinch when his leg accidentally brushed against hers. She wouldn't look in his direction, and he could see Chris giving them both the once-over. Shon was oblivious to the tension between the two, but Chris was observant and could tell there was something in the air. A look passed between Terry and Chris that all but said "we will talk later". Chris had warned him about fucking with Kayla, but he had allowed his other head to get him into trouble.

Kayla couldn't wait to get away from Terry and South Padre Island. Even though she had not eaten anything all day, food was the last thing on her mind. She could see Terry stealing glances at her out of the corner of his eye, but she pretended to be engrossed in conversation with Jordan and Pharris. In reality, she could have cared less about anything that anyone at the table had to say and would rather be in the hotel room crying her eyes out.

"Ladies, I hate to interrupt your conversation, but Kayla and I need to have a quick conversation outside."

Kayla could not believe that Terry had the audacity to interrupt the conversation with her girls. She had absolutely nothing else to say to him. He had basically told her that she needed to forget all about having sex with him and pretend like everything was all honkie dorie. But he knew he had her backed into a corner. She was not going to allow him to push her into making a scene, so, with a plastered grin on her face, she followed him to the front of the restaurant.

"What could you possibly have to say to me?" Kayla said defiantly once the two were out of earshot.

"That I'm sorry and that I don't want to ruin your trip. Let's just make it through this last day. I don't like seeing you upset."

Kayla rolled her eyes. "You don't like seeing me upset, but you treat me like a piece of ass. How sweet of you!" She had just about had enough of men acting like they gave a damn. Actions spoke louder than words.

"Stop being so damn stubborn. You don't want the drama that comes along with this situation, no more than I do."

"Don't tell me what the fuck I want."

"Kayla, you know absolutely nothing about me."

"But I want to know."

Terry looked down at Kayla's impatient stare. He couldn't understand his inner need to keep her happy.

"Let's talk more about this tonight. Put a smile on your face, and don't let me ruin your last day here."

Kayla hated to admit that he was right. This was supposed to be her getaway trip, and she would be a fool to let Terry ruin it. His cousin had done enough damage for the both of them. She took a deep breath and turned to walk back into the restaurant, but Terry pulled her back by her hand.

"Let me see you smile," he told her as he turned her chin up to his face.

"I will smile when I'm away from you," she sarcastically sang out as she pulled away from his hold on her chin.

"Kayla, I will dunk your ass over that pier," he said, signaling to the pier that ran along the back of the restaurant with his eyes. "Smile, so that I know we are going to be able to go back in there and enjoy ourselves."

"Kiss my ass."

"Your ass is what landed us in this predicament."

Kayla couldn't help but laugh out loud. And with that, Terry grabbed her shoulders and turned her towards the restaurant. She wanted to continue to pout, but realized that she had already lost the battle.

"What did you two have to talk about?" Jordan asked as Kayla and Terry approached the table. "We've been waiting on you mofos to order."

"Terry was just schooling me on dog-ass men," Kayla replied, picking up the menu. She grimaced as he pinched her thigh under the table and tried to keep her casual appearance.

"Uh-huh," Pharris replied, trying to catch Kayla's eyes. She knew better.

The group ordered and ate their fill, and then all went their separate ways. Since this was everyone's last night together in South Padre, each couple had made special plans to spend the last night alone. Terry decided to take Kayla back to his place, so they could reach an amicable decision about their situation in private. He dropped Kayla back off at her resort, so she could gather her bags, since she would not be returning to the resort before leaving for the airport the next day.

Once back in her hotel suite, Kayla gathered her things that were thrown all over the place and did a bag check to make sure she was not missing anything. She had packed like she was going away for a week, so she hoped that she had not mistakenly left any of her expensive garments hidden anywhere. Pharris and Jordan walked in minutes after her, but they could sense her ambivalence about talking about Terry. The two knew she would talk when she was ready.

After loading her bags and placing them by the front door, she ran a bath for the last time in this suite, and thoroughly washed every inch of her body with her Victoria's Secret Love Spell shower gel. Even though sex was not on the menu, Kayla still wanted to leave her fragrance behind after she was gone.

Following her bath, Kayla dressed quickly in a pair of Victoria's Secret Pink collection sweats in turquoise. She threw the matching zip front hoodie on over a small cami that showed her flat stomach and pierced belly. She had thought about wearing lingerie to tempt Terry into one last tryst, but had decided against it. The last thing she needed was to have to deal with anymore rejection from this man she was so attracted to. As Kayla was pulling on her Ugg boots and zipping up her coat, the phone in her suite began to ring.

"Madam, there is someone here to pick you up."

Kayla instructed the front desk receptionist to send a bellhop to bring her bags down, and, after giving herself the once over in the mirror, she hurried down to meet Terry. As Kayla alighted from the elevator, to her surprise, standing in the lobby of the La Copa was Dareon, holding a bouquet of roses. Kayla could feel herself breathing slowly, as her chest constricted. *What the fuck is he doing here? And what if Terry comes while he is here?*

"What are you doing here? And how did you find out where I was?" Kayla asked Dareon as she approached him cautiously.

"I miss you, and your mother told me where you were. It's a good thing you keep her out of our business. And, Kayla, by the way, I forgive you."

"Forgive me for what?" Kayla asked, praying that he did not know about her and Terry. It was none of his business.

"For fucking up my truck, of course, because, thanks to you, I have a brand new one."

Dareon's last comment made Kayla remember the reason she was down here in the first place— because *he* had fucked up, not her. She had no reason to feel guilty, and would be damned if his cheating ass rained on her parade.

"Thanks for caring enough to come down here, Dareon, and breaking your cheating habits for a day, but you can keep the fucking flowers. I was just on my way out, and I would appreciate it if you would let me leave without making a scene. But I am prepared to start screaming if you try and follow me out the door."

Kayla shot Dareon a look of disgust as she walked past him and out the front of the resort. *Terry, please come before he comes out after me,* she silently prayed.

As if sent by God, she watched as Terry wheeled his Denali directly in front of the La Copa Resort. Kayla signaled for the bellhop to hurriedly load her bags as she constantly looked over her shoulder for Dareon. After making sure the coast was clear, she hopped into Terry's truck, and they rode off into the night.

"Terry, he is here."

"What do you mean by 'he is here', Kayla?" Terry said as he abruptly pulled the truck over to the side of the rode and came to a complete stop, causing Kayla to glance behind them for oncoming traffic.

It was a good thing it was off-peak season in South Padre, because there was not another car in sight.

"Dareon. He surprised me at the resort. I came downstairs thinking it was you."

"How in the fuck did he find out where you were?"

"My mother. She didn't mean any harm, though. She probably thought he was coming to surprise me or something. I try to keep her out of my relationship when things get really bad between me and Dareon."

"And this is the shit I told you about. I'm taking you back."

"No, Terry. Please, just let us enjoy tonight. I came down here to get away from the drama. Please! Let's just enjoy tonight, and I will handle it. I don't want you involved any more than you have to be in me and Dareon's drama."

"Kayla, wise the fuck up! This shit is fucked up. I fucked my cousin's girl. This shit is not going to just blow over. I am risking my family behind this bullshit."

Kayla burst into tears. "Just tell me what you want me to do, and I will do it. I can't deal with this shit right now. Why can't I just be happy?"

Terry reached over and lifted Kayla's chin with his thumb, so she could face him. "I can't stand to see you cry, but just know that this shit is all the way fucked up."

"I just don't want to worry about that right now. Can we please just go to your place?"

Terry eased the car back onto the Main Street and headed to the beach house that he and his boys owned, but only spent about three weeks out of the year in. They had hired a cleaning crew to keep the place immaculate throughout the year, and let family members use it when they were in South Padre, just to keep the place occupied.

Terry pulled his car into the circular drive, and then walked around to the passenger side to open the door for Kayla. He handed her the house key, as he unloaded her overnight bag and carried it in.

From the moment Kayla stuck her key in the door and entered the house, she was in love. The front door opened into a small,quaint living room equipped with an already lit fireplace, a circular sofa, and a 62" plasma TV that was installed above the fireplace next to an impressive DVD collection. The entire place was furnished with contemporary furniture in different hues of red and black, and looked as if it was decorated right out of a home décor Magazine.

"My mother decorated when we first got this place," Terry explained as he watched the expression on Kayla's face.

"It's beautiful." Kayla said as she kneeled to lay on a rug that was spread out in front of the fireplace.

She had always wanted to make love in front of a fireplace, but, oh, well, that would have to wait for another night, because she was going to do everything in her power to keep her legs closed tonight. Terry left her bag in the foyer and tried to resist taking her on the rug. They needed to talk, and that was part of the only reason he'd agreed to bring her to his place alone. Instead of joining her on the rug, he took a seat on the sofa.

"Kayla, come here," Terry said, patting the cushion next to him.

He didn't need any additional temptations added tonight. He just wanted to talk and show Kayla to one of the guest bedrooms. It was turning into a long weekend.

Kayla reluctantly took the seat next to him. *Straight to business...*She was not looking forward to this conversation.

"I don't want you to leave here feeling like a piece of ass. I can be honest and say I'm really feeling you, but you and I both know the deal. Dareon is family, and you're his girl. It is what it is, straight like that."

"So, that's it? You could have called the hotel for this conversation."

"You deserve more than that."

"But I don't deserve you?"

Terry looked at Kayla. There was so much that he wanted to say, but he didn't feel like any of it actually mattered. It did not matter that he was more attracted to her than he had been to any female....*since Samantha.* It didn't matter that he was drawn to her wittiness and ambition. It didn't matter that she had been on his mind since Dallas. All that mattered was that she belonged to Dareon.

"Kayla, look. In my life, loyalty is more important than..."

"And what is your life? I am tired of hearing about how much I don't know about you."

Terry wrapped up the short version of his life in less than five minutes. There were just some things that were not made for conversations. He was comfortable enough to tell her his true occupation, but she did not need to know the gory details that were his reality. Truth was, loyalty was something that he had no problem killing over and had killed over.

"So, I am supposed to be intimidated because you sell drugs?" Kayla looked at him with a blank stare.

She might have grown up in an affluent home, but she had always been drawn to bad boys.

Terry knew that Kayla wouldn't understand the scale of his business, but it was not for him to explain. He would just allow her to continue to compare him to the local weed dealers she had categorized him with. He was a million dollar nigga, but that really was neither here nor there.

"Kayla, let me show you to your room. This situation is not about to become more fucked up."

Terry stood up abruptly. The sheer rejection in his voice left Kayla sitting there awestruck. She wanted Terry and refused to believe that his words reflected his true feelings.

"I am not sleeping here if I'm not going to be sleeping with you. So, you can just take me back to the La Copa."

Terry was the one taken aback this time. He hadn't thought that she would want to go back to the resort, and he knew in the back of his head that he wanted her to stay there with him. For a second, they stared each other down. She crossed her arms.

"Since you haven't moved to grab your keys, I am going to assume that you agree with me," she said.

Then, she began to remove her boots.

Kayla could smell defeat from across the room, but she hadn't won just yet. She watched Terry spin on his heels and walk down a dark hallway. In mere seconds, he came back carrying an oversized blanket and two pillows.

"I guess we won't be sleeping tonight then. And just in case you doze, here's your pillow," he said, tossing a pillow at her head. Kayla couldn't help but to laugh. At least, she was partially getting her way.

"Now, pick out a movie." Terry gestured towards his extensive movie collection.

He sat on the sofa and watched Kayla as she scanned through the DVD collection. *She is bad as hell*, he thought as he watched her perfectly manicured fingers skim down each DVD carefully as she contemplated over which movie to watch.

"Ohhh, my favorite," Kayla said as she pulled *A Low Down Dirty Shame* from the DVD rack.

"What you know about that?" Terry said as he got up from his comfortable position to help her load the DVD into the surround sound system.

"Coffee is good with crème, but better when it's black," Kayla said as she imitated her favorite scene in the movie where Damon Wayans pretended to be gay.

Terry laughed at her accurate depiction. She had enacted the part down to the mannerisms Damon had used to deceive Raymond's white lover. As they laid on opposite ends of the sofa and watched the film, laughing throughout most of it, Kayla decided to ask Terry a question that had been bothering her ever since their initial meeting at the family reunion.

"Who is Samantha?" Kayla asked, breaking the silence that had lingered between them. She didn't want the night to pass with their obvious attraction being marred by a movie and spacing on a sofa.

Terry paused, placing the TV on mute. He, then, signaled for her to join him on his end of the sofa. Kayla's heart fluttered as she moved towards him. "Samantha was my ex-girlfriend. She overdosed a couple of years ago."

"Sorry for asking," Kayla said, laying her head on his chest. She was surprised when he wrapped his arms around her.

"Naw, you straight," Terry replied. "She got hooked on the shit I was selling, and, no matter how many times I tried to get her help, she just kept using. We were high school sweethearts. She had everything going for her, and one day, she decided to try my stash when I wasn't around."

"You don't have to tell me."

"But I want to. I kept ignoring all the signs that she had a problem till one time I brought her to the family reunion, and out of nowhere, her nose just started bleeding." Terry paused to gather his thoughts as Kayla just sat in silence and listened. "I tried over and over again to get her help." Kayla could hear his voice harden as he became more emotional while telling her of his heartbreak. "But every time she got out of rehab, within weeks, she was using again. Then, she got pregnant, and I pleaded with her to stop using, if not for us, then for our child. She stayed clean for about two months, and then started using again right under my nose. I didn't even know she had started back using until she gave birth to a stillborn. That bitch killed our baby. She was a functional cocaine addict. She could be high as a kite, but still function as if she was just as normal as you and me. I thought about getting out of the game and moving away to save her, but, after the death of our baby boy, I threw her out onto the streets. She was found dead a few weeks later."

Kayla turned around to face Terry. She could see the raw pain that was still in his eyes. She couldn't resist tracing the outline of his chiseled face with her lips. She would never hurt him like his ex. He didn't push her away. Instead, Terry adjusted his position to wrap Kayla's legs around him and unzipped her hoodie. He, then, removed that along with her cami and began to suck on her already hardened nipples. Kayla masked her moans with kisses to his neck.

"Terry, let's just forget about Dareon," she pleaded.

"I just want to feel you," Terry whispered in her ear as he removed her sweatpants to reveal her bare bottom.

As if possessed, Kayla found herself hurriedly unbuttoning Terry's jeans as she ground against his hardening dick while he sucked on her neck. As soon as Kayla had Terry's jeans and boxers off and on the floor next to her pile of clothes, she pulled off his shirt and straddled him. Terry grabbed her ass as she rode him up and down, using her vaginal muscles to squeeze his dick, while she moaned loudly in pleasure. As she rode him, Terry bucked to meet her stride, making her go crazy as her first orgasm hit her like a wave. Unable to stop, Terry pulled Kayla onto the rug in front of the fireplace and watched her naked figure as she bounced up and down on his dick, her shadow moving with the flicker of the flames. As they made love over and over in front of the fireplace, neither of them saw the figure staring at them through the living room window.

Chapter 10

"Hurry! I have to be at the airport in an hour," Kayla fussed as she waited for Terry to lock the house, so he could take her to the airport. Since she didn't have her phone, she had to rely on Terry to wake her up early enough to catch her flight, but that had turned out to be a joke. Terry woke Kayla up at the last minute, and he was now taking his time, sauntering over to the truck to drive her to the airport in nearby Brownsville.

"You shouldn't have kept me up all night," Terry leaned in and kissed her on the lips as he started the truck.

"You are a grown ass man and could have said no," Kayla said as she stuck her tongue out at him. "I know that my stuff is good, but damn."

"It's the best, baby," Terry replied as he sped across the bridge to get Kayla to the airport on time.

Kayla had thought about purposely missing her flight to spend more time with Terry, but the next flight did not leave till late that night, and she needed to study for her Monday morning classes. On the way to the airport, Kayla did a mental checklist in her head to make sure she had everything. It wasn't guaranteed that she was going to see Terry again, and she didn't want to risk leaving anything at his house. The thought that he was just a South Padre Island fling made her lightheaded.

Terry heard her deep sigh and couldn't resist grabbing her hand over the console.

"Stop stressing over this situation, Kayla. We both had a great time, and we can just leave it at that."

Kayla didn't say anything. What else could possibly be said? Once again, she longed to be at home in the solace of her own bedroom to deal with her torrent of emotions. The drive to the airport was turning out to be bitter sweet.

Terry pulled up to the airport in more than enough time for Kayla to go through security and luggage check-in before she boarded the plane. "Can you give me a call, so that I know you made it back safely?"

Almost as soon as the words left Terry's mouth, he began to regret them. This situation needed to stay in South Padre, and he was allowing her to contact him from Baton Rouge.

"I don't have your number," Kayla replied in a low voice. "And I left my phone at home."

Terry found a slip of paper and pen in his truck. He quickly jotted down his number and handed it to her.

"Have a safe flight, Kayla," he said, turning her chin to face him.

Kayla couldn't resist the urge to kiss him one last time. She noticed that he did not resist, but instead grabbed the back of her head and deepened their kiss. It was she who pulled away.

There was nothing else that needed to be said. They had both had a great time in South Padre, and it was time for her to return home to her drama with Dareon.

"Let me get your bags, Kayla." Terry broke the silence and hopped out of the truck.

Neither of them wanted to leave each other's presence, but it was for the best. Kayla opened her door and followed Terry to the airport entrance. They exchanged her bags in silence, and Terry gave her a quick, awkward hug before heading back to his illegally parked truck.

Just as he went to open his driver's side door, he heard a voice from behind him say, "So, you fucking my girl now?"

Terry turned around to face a pissed off Dareon. Clearly, Dareon had been waiting at the airport and was now fuming with anger.

"Now is not the time or the place…If you want to talk to me, Dareon, follow me back to the island," Terry told Dareon as he nodded toward all the border patrol officers monitoring the airport, and the two black males in luxury vehicles, holding what seemed to be a hostile conversation, would only draw their attention.

"Naw, fuck that, playboy," Dareon said. "Just know you gonna get yours."

Dareon hopped into his rented Lexus and sped off. *I flew all the way down here for this ungrateful bitch, and she fucks my cousin.* As he sped back towards the island at break-neck speed, he dialed the one person he could confide in, who always had his back.

"Say, Ma. It's me, and you won't believe this shit."

****

After Kayla turned over her bags, and passed through security, she reunited with her girls as they waited for boarding to begin for their flight.

"So, what did you girls do last night?" Kayla asked Jordan and Pharris as they all sipped sodas while seated in the airport lobby.

"I'm assuming the same thing you did," Jordan said smartly as she pointed out a passion mark on Kayla's neck.

Blushing, Kayla popped the collar of her Polo and lightly pushed Jordan.

"What did you do, Pharris?"

"Me and Mr. Can't Eat Pussy spent the night down here in Brownsville because there was a fair down here last night. And no, I did not give him any," Pharris said as she flipped through a magazine.

As the girls sat and gossiped, Kayla told them about how Dareon had showed up at the hotel, and how she was unsure about whether he had seen her leave with Terry. The girls sat up and amused themselves with stories of the weekend until their flight was called for boarding. As the girls stood in line, Jordan's phone began to ring noisily.

"Kayla, it's for you," Jordan told her with a raised eyebrow.

"Dareon was at the airport when I dropped you off, he claims to know what's up. But just holla at me when you make it back to BR," Terry said and immediately disconnected.

As Kayla regained her place in line to board the plane, she instantly got a headache. This situation was all fucked up. She knew that, as soon as Dareon made it back to Baton Rouge, there would be a confrontation about Terry. She had spent the whole weekend screwing around with her boyfriend's cousin, a cousin whom she was sure had hos in every corner of Houston. *Why in the hell would a man as fine as Terry want to be with his cousin's girlfriend who so willingly let him sample her goods all within a weekend?* Kayla rummaged in her purse for a Tylenol pm, swallowed the tiny pill with no water, and chose to spend the entire flight in slumber.

When the girls landed in New Orleans, it was pouring down raining. *Perfect weather to match my mood,* Kayla thought as the trio gathered their bags and headed to the long term parking lot to retrieve Jordan's car. The whole way back to Baton Rouge, Kayla laid in the backseat in a glum mood. Since it was raining and everyone in the vehicle was tired, no one bothered her as she sat in the backseat and sulked. She made up her mind that tonight she would just go to Dareon's house, so, when he got home, she would already be there to get this conversation done and over. What was there to say besides it was over? Why should she continue to be unhappy while he screwed every bitch under the sun and even had a baby on the way? Terry was really not the issue. The issue was that she was done being with someone that clearly preferred to be single.

When Jordan pulled up into their parking garage, Kayla took her bags into the apartment and checked her cell. She had several missed calls and text messages, more than half were from Dareon, but she wasn't in a talking mood. As she unpacked, she first called her mom to inform her that she had made it back safely and then dialed Terry.

"Just calling to let you know I made it back."

"Cool. Have you talked to Dareon?"

"Not yet."

"I told you what could happen. But let me know if that nigga gets outta line. I will still bust his ass."

Kayla liked hearing the aggression in Terry's voice, but she knew he was only speaking out of guilt. He didn't want Dareon to hurt her, but that didn't mean he wanted her either.

"Yeah, I will. Have a safe trip whenever you head back," She replied glumly. South Padre had been fun, and it was over. Now, it was time to deal with something that actually mattered…Dareon.

Chapter 11

So, what's really the deal with you and Kayla?"

It had been hours since the girls had left South Padre, and Chris and Terry were grabbing a bite to eat at Las Americas, a popular local restaurant that served TexMex cuisine.

"To be honest, I couldn't even tell you. I really feel her, but she's Dareon's girl. I would kind of rather just say fuck this and leave the situation in South Padre."

Chris could tell that Terry had a lot more on his mind, but he knew that Terry was a man of few words. Even when Samantha's drug habit had hit the fan, Terry would only give minimal details. Chris didn't even know that Samantha had overdosed until months after it happened. That was a hard blow for everyone to swallow.

Samantha and Terry had been "the" hood couple, and everyone had been shocked and appalled when she had gotten hooked on that shit. Within a matter of months, the ravishing Samantha that was often confused with the hood rapper Rasheeda, had gone from being a 32-24-37 to barely being able to keep up a size 0. Right before the pregnancy, it had gotten to a point that even Chris was ashamed to be seen out in public with Terry and Samantha. According to Terry, Samantha was a functional drug addict, but the rest of the hood knew that she was just the common cracked out bitch that still thought she was on top.

****

Kayla pulled into Dareon's parking garage and sat with her hands clutching the steering wheel. There were a million places that she wanted to be besides Dareon's condo. But it was time to close this chapter in her life and move on to another one. She was grateful that Dareon would not be home for a couple of hours since the next flight leaving South Padre was for late that evening. *I hope he didn't get a private plane,* Kayla thought as she used her key to enter his condo.

Just as her foot was crossing the threshold, Kayla was bum rushed into the condo. She barely had time to catch her footing before her assailant tackled her to the ground. Kayla wanted to scream, but it felt like her voice was lodged in her throat. She was able to escape his grasp long enough to get to her feet and rush down the hall towards Dareon's bedroom.

The man clad in all black with the build of a retired linebacker was quick on his feet, and Kayla was within feet of the bedroom when he struck. Kayla felt pressure and rough hands around her neck as she was hurled against the wall. The crushing impact caused her tiny frame to collapse onto the hard wooden floors.

"Let me go please," Kayla called out in a barely audible whisper, while trying to recover her breath from her collision with the floor. The pain in her elbow made her want to cry out in agony. "Take whatever you want."

She saw the man's foot lift quickly above her rib cage before she felt the excruciating pain in her side. This was her first time on the receiving end of an ass whooping, and the aches in her side and elbow were agonizing.

Again, Kayla watched the heavy boot lift in the air. This time, she lifted her arms, grabbed his foot, and did her best to throw him off balance. *That move worked in Enough,* she briefly thought as she watched the man stumble to regain his footing. But he was much quicker than Kayla, and her attempt to derail his attack only increased his fury.

"Stupid bitch!" he yelled out as he delivered a swift kick that struck Kayla in her back.

"Arghhhh!" she screamed out, unable to take the pain that radiated down her spine. Tears streamed down her face, and the fear that this might be the end of her life made her want to keep fighting. *Why hasn't anyone called the police?*

Kayla was not prepared when her legs were swiftly lifted into the air, and the intruder proceeded to drag her down the hallway. *He's heading towards Dareon's room.*

"Don't you dare scream, or I will kill you," he snapped, reading her mind.

Kayla wiggled to get free of his iron clad grasp on her ankles, but her struggle was futile. She was roughly lifted from the ground and flipped onto the bed. *Please don't let him rape me.* Kayla cringed at the thought. It was time to keep fighting. As soon as he released her, Kayla mustered her strength and flew at him like a savage. But the man's meaty hands hastily took hold of her throat and began to squeeze. As Kayla gagged and kicked at her masked attacker, she could feel the room darken as her head begun to spin. Her consciousness had just begun to slip away when, all of a sudden, the pressure was released.

Kayla heard the commotion, before she saw the flurry of fists. Her vision was still blurry, but she recognized Dareon's form raining blow after blow on her attacker.

"Call the police, Dareon! Please stop! You might kill him," she whispered hoarsely.

Kayla, in a state of delirium, tried to lift herself from the bed but instead knocked the bedside lamp over. It was the noise of the shattering lamp that snapped Dareon out of his trance.

Dareon pressed his knee into the chest of the unconscious assailant and retrieved his cell from his pocket. Within minutes of calling the police, Kayla's unmasked attacker was placed into the back of a police car and hauled off to the parish jail. As soon as the police finished taking Kayla's statement and left her and Dareon alone, she collapsed into Dareon's arms. The investigating officer had advised her to come to the station to make an official statement, but that was the furthest thing from her mind.

"He almost killed me. I could feel myself slipping away," Kayla cried, close to panicking.

"It's okay, baby. I'm here." Dareon held Kayla until her sobs subsided and her trembling ceased. She had vehemently refused to allow the paramedics to take her to the hospital, and the dark red lines around her neck had him worried. Dareon was genuinely glad that he had walked in when he did, because, if he'd come in even a few seconds later, the assailant could have killed Kayla. He sent a silent prayer up that he had decided last minute to have his mother send the private jet, instead of waiting for his late night flight.

Neither of them recognized the intruder, and the police assumed this was just a case of a robbery gone badly. The attacker had managed to avoid the video cameras in the parking garage and in the building, and it was very possible that the true victim of the crime was supposed to be Dareon. From the police's standpoint, Kayla had just been at the wrong place at the wrong time.

Dareon stroked and kneaded Kayla's back in a slow, methodic rhythm. Her knees were clutched to her chest in her upright position on the sofa, and Dareon had encased her body in his muscular arms. As much as Kayla despised

Dareon's cheating habits, she was thankful that he had stopped the attack. Her ribs felt bruised, and she had a throbbing headache, but she was alive. That was all that mattered.

"Kayla, let's get some rest. It's been a long night, bae."

They had been sitting on the couch since Kayla's interview with the detective, and it had been a long day for both of them. Kayla didn't refuse when Dareon lifted her weary frame into his arms and carried her into his bedroom.

The words that she had practiced the whole drive over didn't matter in that moment. All that she wanted to do was to snuggle in Dareon's arms and feel protected from any harm.

Throughout the entire night, Dareon held Kayla as she continuously woke up in cold sweats. She kept waking up, kicking and screaming, fighting Dareon, until he was able to calm her down enough for her to realize she was safe. Dareon and Kayla both missed their Monday morning classes.

Around noon, Kayla finally pulled herself out of bed and decided that she, at least, needed to call her mom to let someone know about the attack. She was still pretty shaken up and needed to discuss the incident with someone besides Dareon. As Kayla retrieved her phone from her purse and walked into the living room, her indicator light flashed, signaling that she had three new voicemails. One was from Jordan, one was from her mother, and, surprisingly, there was another from Dareon's mother, Nicole. Nicole rarely ever called her phone, and she couldn't imagine what the woman could want this time. The last time Nicole had called her phone, she had ended up back with Dareon. After the drama from the previous night, Kayla decided to call Nicole back later, rather than sooner. Instead, she dialed her mother.

Kayla tried to keep the details about the attack as brief as possible, so she would't worry her mother too much, and she put much emphasis on the fact that the attacker was now in jail. But being a parent, Kayla's mother made arrangements to fly into Baton Rouge the next day to at least see with her own eyes that her only child was okay.

Mrs. Davis knew Kayla always tried to act strong in every situation no matter how strenuous it was, but, as far as she was concerned, Kayla was going to counseling ASAP. The last thing that she wanted was for her baby to be scarred for life behind this incident. And as much as Kayla resisted her mother having to fly all the way from Houston, in the back of her head, she was relieved that she was coming. At least, now she wouldn't have to sleep alone for a couple of nights. Kayla was grateful that Dareon had saved her life, but she still had to deal with the issue she had initially been there to resolve.

"Dareon, we need to talk," Kayla said as she walked back into the bedroom and sat on the edge of the bed.

"I already know you were with Terry in South Padre. I saw you leave the hotel with him, but I ain't even trippin', though. You got caught up in a weak moment. I understand, shit happens. I know you can't think that he's about to wife your ass." Dareon watched himself on ESPN as he spoke, not even caring to glance at Kayla.

He was so used to her "it's over" speeches that he doubted this one would be any different. So what, she had probably let his cousin hit it…

Kayla stared at Dareon in disbelief. The more she was around him lately, the more she realized he was a pompous asshole. The gratefulness she felt in her heart went out the window in a flash, and she realized that it was time to handle her business.

"You know what, Dareon? It has been three years too long. Thanks for showing me what kind of man I don't need in my life. I'm better off without your dog ass. Good luck with Samara and the baby situation. I hope she takes your ass for every penny you will ever be worth. Goodbye, Dareon."

With that said, Kayla tossed Dareon his house key, and made sure to slam his front door behind her. The last thing she heard him say on her way into a new and brighter future was, "Bitch, don't forget I saved your life."

Kayla could not believe his ass, and, as she drove out of his parking garage and past his new white Escalade, it crossed her mind to fuck up his vehicle again. *It will hurt him more when he realizes that I'm really done,* she thought as she smirked to herself. And one thing was for sure, Mommy's money wouldn't be able to buy his no-good ass a new ego.

Kayla sped out of Dareon's parking garage at full speed. The feeling of liberation that vibrated through her soul made a smile creep across her face. As she sped through the college campus to her residence, she couldn't resist calling Terry. Even though she hated to admit it, Dareon's comment about her being a piece of ass bothered her to her core.

"Hey! Did you make it back to Houston?" she asked, relieved that he'd answered.

"About an hour away. You good?"

For a brief second, Kayla wanted to tell him about the attack. However, that thought went as fast as it had come. The last thing that she needed was sympathy from someone that probably had one hundred girlfriends in Houston.

"I'm fine. Just making sure you made it back safely."

"A'ight then. I will text you once I hit the city limits."

"Wait. What do you think about me coming to Houston this weekend?"

The words left Kayla's lips before she could even think to retract them. She slammed her hand to her forehead and couldn't believe that she was showing her vulnerabilities. *Damn! He's going to think I am a loser. He just saw me.*

"I think you can do whatever you want. What are you really asking me?"

Kayla hesitated and allowed a couple of seconds to pass before answering.

"I kind of want to see you." *There. I said it.*

The deafening silence on the other end of the phone made her instantly regret her response. She did not know him well enough to know whether his silence was an indicator of his annoyance or deep contemplation.

"Let me see what I have up for the weekend, and I will let you know."

Kayla couldn't help but to feel slightly rejected. She was grateful when he told her that he would call her back. *Maybe, Dareon was right after all....*

Chapter 12

D*areon, the game, Samantha*…All three of those things were reason enough for Terry to leave Kayla alone and not put anymore thought into their chemistry. But as Terry lay poolside at his home, Kayla kept appearing in his thoughts. *What was it about Dareon's girlfriend that got him going?*

Kayla was bad in every since of the word, but so was the Brazilian chick swimming naked in his pool. Bad bitches came a dime a dozen to niggas like Terry, and he couldn't understand why he was sweating his cousin's girl so hard. Terry was used to girls throwing themselves at him for the chance of snagging a baller, but he had never felt the instantaneous connection he felt with Kayla…*at least, not since Samantha.* The thought of Samantha snapped Terry from his trance. She was reason enough to forget all about Kayla.

Deep down, Terry knew that he still felt responsible for Samantha's demise. Samantha had always been straight-laced, until she fell head over heels for Terry. She had begged him to leave Houston and move with her to Indiana for college, but he had refused. She had the full ride to Purdue, not him. Terry had barely skated through high school and the thrill of the fast money he made in Houston had his heart.

Instead of pursuing her long distance college dreams, Samantha enrolled in the University of Houston to stay near Terry. More than a handful of times, she had threatened to leave, but those threats usually fell upon Terry's deaf ears. As far as he was concerned, he was able to provide everything their hearts desired, so nothing else really mattered. Terry knew that four years of college couldn't have provided either of them with the crib, luxury vehicles, expensive vacations, and shopping sprees that hustling provided. It was his refusal to leave the game and her desire for attention that led her to try his product. He thought back to their first argument about her addiction.

Samantha had walked in the house in the wee hours of the morning glossy-eyed and barely coherent. He smelled the alcohol reeking from her pores, before she saw him sitting in a chair in their bedroom awaiting her arrival. In his hand, he clutched a letter from the University of Houston that was the equivalent of her walking papers. He had made excuses for her and paid her tuition when she lost her scholarship the semester prior, but the devil was now staring him in the face. The rumors were true. His girlfriend was a certified cokehead.

"Baby, why are you sitting in the dark?"

Terry could barely stand the sight of the giggling, discombobulated form reaching for him in the dark.

"What the fuck is this shit, Samantha? I hustle all day, so you can have whatever your heart desires. And you get hooked on that shit? I could kill you."

"Oh, everybody does it. You don't mind it when you're out there selling it to other people. I just want to have fun. It's not like you're ever here with me."

It took everything in him not to choke her on sight. Instead, he rose from his seat and turned on the bedroom light, holding the letter in front of her eyes.

"Is this what the fuck you meant by having fun? You have been kicked out of school, and I am three seconds away from kicking your ass. You have two fuckin' choices: get clean or get the fuck out."

And that began a year of treatment programs and relapses that seemingly came back to back. Samantha would never stay the full term at any treatment center and would prey on Terry's guilt to bring her back home. Each time, she would swear she was clean. And each time, she would be back to using within the month. And then she got pregnant. Terry thought that, if anything could save her, it was going to be their son.

Terrence Jaylen Carver Jr. was stillborn May 1st, 2005 at 9:17 A.M. The doctors had said that, TJ, as Terry had already nicknamed him, had been dead for quite a while before the emergency cesarean. Samantha had not even noticed that the child she was carrying had stopped moving. That had been the straw that broke the camel's back, and, even still, Terry couldn't put into words the anguish that had torn him apart a day at a time for months.

The first and only time that he had ever put his hands on a woman had been the day that Samantha had been released from the hospital. Instead of celebrating the joyous homecoming of their child, he had to deal with the indifferent attitude of his cokehead girlfriend. When she strolled into the house already high and glossy-eyed, he lost it. The thought of her still snorting coke when there was a $30,000 nursery upstairs that would never be used sent him into a dangerous rage.

It had been Chris that walked in and stopped the brutal ass whooping he had bestowed on Samantha. For two days, he had sat and binge drank and waited for her to return home and join his mourning. Instead, she had found a way to her next high. The streets knew that there was no hell like Terry's fury, but Samantha had never felt his wrath until that moment.

While Chris helped Samantha gather her belongings, Terry caught the next flight out of Houston. That trip had turned into a three month hiatus, while Shon and Chris held down the fort. He didn't stay in any place longer than one week and had spent every waking moment running from his problems. It wasn't until he reached Australia that he decided to return home. Thankfully, he returned to an empty house with fresh locks on the doors and word that Samantha's supplier had been found with a bullet in between his eyes.

The hardest part had been walking into what should have been TJ's nursery, only to find that it had been converted into a guest room without any remnants of the grandiose space that it had once been. The $20,000 Majestic Carriage crib fit for a prince and matching custom made dresser had been replaced with a queen bed set, and the pale blue paint had been changed to a dark mocha.

"Papi, come and join me in the pool."

The angelic voice snapped Terry out of his trip down memory lane. He rarely thought about Samantha, but, since meeting Kayla, those painful memories had surfaced twice. Maybe, his house guest could take his mind off both.

****

Kayla awoke from a sleepless midday nap and couldn't help but to check her phone. *No text from Terry.* Even though she wasn't surprised, she was still slightly bothered. It had been hours since he told her he was almost to Houston. As she glanced around her darkened bedroom, Kayla realized just how much she needed a break from Baton Rouge. A week ago, it had been Dareon cheating, and, now, she was being forced to deal with her vicious attack. *Maybe, it makes more sense to go home this weekend,* Kayla thought as she picked up her cell to text her mother.

"Mom, don't book your flight. I'm coming home this weekend."

Secretly, Kayla hoped that she would see Terry in Houston, but she didn't get her hopes up. Lately, her love life had been nothing but one big letdown after another.

Kayla rolled out of bed and walked into the dark hallway that led to their living room. The house was dead silent. *Where are Jordan and Pharris?* After checking each of her roommates' bedrooms and finding them deserted, she called Pharris. Kayla still had not told them about the attack and didn't want them to be alarmed at her appearance. The knot on her forehead and the red bruises around her neck spoke volumes.

"Where are you, and is Jordan with you?"

"No, I am at the library studying. I have been trying to call Jordan since earlier. I don't know where her ass is."

"A'ight, let me call her. I have something I need to tell both of y'all together. See you when you get home."

Kayla disconnected and tried calling Jordan. Her phone immediately went to voicemail. Instead of leaving one though, she decided to take a long bath to gather her thoughts. She would try calling Jordan again when she got out the tub. This past weekend had been long and draining, and it was nice to have a moment to herself. Before Kayla knew it, she had dozed off in the hot, sudsy water.

Kayla awoke to voices and laughter coming through the front door. *It sounds like Jordan, but who is the baritone?* Kayla quickly hopped out of the now cold water and put on her robe before peeping her head into the hallway to see who Jordan had brought home. Kayla cracked her bedroom door, and almost fainted. Posed in front of her door, about to knock, was Terry.

"What are you doing here?"

"Chris wanted to come fuck with Jordan, so he asked me to hop on the G5 with him. I wasn't doing anything else, so…Wait! What the fuck is wrong with your neck?"

Kayla really was speechless. She was excited to see him, but confused at the same time. *Didn't he say that there could be nothing between them since she dated Dareon? So, why is he here? Couldn't Chris have come alone?* A million questions ran through her head and almost made her forget the question that he was standing there waiting for an answer to. *Oooo…*She hadn't even had a chance to tell her roommates what happened, and here was Terry demanding answers with a scowl on his face.

Instead of answering, she looked down at the ground. She was almost ashamed that her decision to spend the night with Dareon had led to her attack. *The robber had to be after Dareon, right?*

"Kayla, look at me. What happened? These marks were not there when I took you to the airport in Padre."

Terry took Kayla's chin in between his fingers and lifted her head to meet his inquisitive gaze. The overwhelming urge to be her protector surfaced again, and he instantly regretted letting Chris talk him into taking this last minute trip. But it was the first time that he had seen his friend so into any female, so he couldn't turn him down. And it wasn't like Shon could just up and leave the city; he had a wife at home. At least, that was what Terry told himself. Secretly, he knew that he wanted to see Kayla, just as bad as Chris wanted to see Jordan. Even Maricella, the Brazilian beauty queen that had let him stick it any hole he wanted to, had not taken his mind off of Kayla.

Kayla remained silent for a few more seconds before taking a deep breath and answering. Terry's dark eyes were mesmerizing, and she could see his concern emanating throughout them as she told him about her attack.

"Have you been back to the police station?"

"Not yet," Kayla admitted, letting her eyes drop back towards the floor. She was waiting for him to chastise her and was genuinely shocked by his answer.

"Good. Don't go. Let me handle this shit. I'm about to go and make a call."

Kayla watched Terry walk out of her bedroom, down the hallway, and out the front door. *What did he mean 'let him handle it'? What is he going to do? He isn't a killer, is he?*

It took Kayla less than three seconds to throw on some baggy sweatpants and a t-shirt before sprinting down the hallway to Jordan's room. She didn't want Terry to get in trouble behind her mess, and she needed to tell Chris to stop him from doing something stupid. She knocked once before opening the door.

"Damn, bitch! Where are your manners?"

Jordan quickly yelled out throwing the comforter over Chris's half naked body. They clearly had not wasted any time getting down to business.

"Terry…my attacker…I don't want him to get into trouble…" Kayla's words came out in a jumbled mess, and she could barely contain her ragged breathing.

"Slow down, Kayla. Don't tell me that Dareon put his hands on you? I swear I will kill that nigga myself," Jordan said, rising from the bed in her bra and panties to rub her distressed roommate's back. Kayla was barely fazed by her roommate's half-naked state, and it took everything to contain her emotions.

"I was attacked at Dareon's, not by Dareon. And Terry just left, saying that he was going to handle it. I don't want him to do anything stupid."

Chris couldn't help but to suppress a chuckle. Kayla was obviously in over her head. Terry was good at making problems disappear like magic. It came along with their line of work.

"Kayla, don't trip. Terry is not going to do anything to get himself any unnecessary jail time. That nigga has too much to lose to go down behind some dumb shit. Calm down, and let that nigga handle his business."

Calm down? Kayla looked at Chris in utter disbelief, and then it hit her. Terry had warned her that she wasn't ready for his life, and maybe he was right. The few hours that she had spent in jail had scared her straight, and she had been thankful her mother had been able to get the disturbing the peace charges dropped.

"Kayla, if you don't want him to be involved, just tell him, even though I think that nigga deserves to get fucked up for hurting you. But, as you can see, Chris and I were kind of in the middle of something."

Kayla wished that Pharris was home to get her point-of-view, but it looked like she was on her own. She issued a quick apology and headed back down the hallway to her bedroom. Terry had still not returned. She wanted to be grateful that he cared, but, deep down, she wondered if he was just protective over any women that had been assaulted by a man. *Stop, Kayla...the what if game never gets you anywhere.*

Kayla sat on her bed and rested her forehead in the palm of her hands. Terry wanted to protect her. *Why should she be concerned about someone that tried to kill her?*

Kayla didn't realize Terry entered the room until he sat on the bed next to her.

"Kayla, let me see your bruises."

She lifted her head and allowed him to gently trace each one with his fingertips. Kayla could feel herself stiffen when he replaced his fingers with his lips. She wanted to grab his face and kiss his lips, but she was afraid that he would stop.

"Terry, stop." Kayla broke from the trance of his soft lips and the quiver that had moved down her spine to between her thighs. She was not going to allow him to get her all hot and bothered, only to push her away again.

"I don't want to."

"Why are you doing this, Terry? You have already made it clear that you don't want me."

Kayla knew her voice was coming out in a whiny whisper, but she could hardly concentrate with his lips on her neck.

"I can't stay away from you."

There they were. The words that she had wanted to hear.

"I want to kill that muthafucka for putting his hands on you."

Kayla turned her head, so that his lips were inches from her own. She never wanted to kiss him more than she did at that moment. It seemed like everything was going in slow motion. The kiss seemed to never end, and it confirmed everything that she already knew about how she felt about him. She wanted Terry and everything that came along with him. *So what if he's a goon? I want him to be my goon.*

It didn't take long for Terry to remove all of Kayla's clothes, and she couldn't help but to admire his beautiful physique as he undressed. Both of his arms were covered in a full sleeve of tattoos, and on his chest was the Serenity prayer from one pec to the other. His six pack was defined, and she couldn't help but follow the defined lines from his sides to the rod pointed in her direction.

"Do you like what you see?"

Kayla couldn't help but to blush.

"Come here," Terry gruffly told Kayla.

She didn't know what he was about to do, but the butterflies in her stomach were anxious with anticipation.

"Bend all the way over and touch your toes."

Kayla followed his instructions and could barely contain her excitement. His kisses up and down her spine were enough to illicit a moan. She wasn't ready when he entered her roughly from behind. She grabbed her ankles and did not care who heard her screams. Terry wrapped one arm around Kayla to help steady her balance and tried his best not to cum. He couldn't believe how wet she was around his piece and the way she was able to grind back onto him. He could feel his balls slapping the back of her jiggling ass, and he sped up his pace. The sound of her moaning and screaming his name was about to drive him insane.

"Lay across the bed."

"No, you lay down," Kayla replied abruptly, pulling from his embrace. It was time to show him what she could do. She gave him just enough time to adjust his position, before she climbed on top of him and slid down. She placed her hands behind her head and began to slow wind. The "O" that his mouth formed was enough to let her know that she was doing her job well.

"You feel so good, Terry," she managed to get out in between moans. "I think I'm about to cum."

Terry could feel his eyes rolling into the back of his head. He didn't want to pull out, but he could feel his nut on the edge. It was time to make her cum. Terry grabbed her ass and began to pump in and out her at a quick pace. When he felt her body slightly convulse, he quickly pulled out.

"I will get a towel," Kayla said breathlessly.

He had definitely put it in her life.

Chapter 13

It took everything for Kayla to get up for class the next morning. Terry had worn her out the night before, and she was surprised that she could still walk. It was almost like his sex drive was insatiable. She didn't even remember falling asleep and wondered whether she had passed out. The sex alone was enough to have her hooked. She didn't want to wake Terry, but she couldn't resist kissing his sleeping eyelids. He didn't even move, and she was secretly amused that he was just as comatose as she had been. She hoped that she would be back from class before he even knew she had left.

Kayla took a quick shower and selected her outfit as silently as she could. Usually, she was dressed for a runway when she left the house, but today her goal was cute and quick. Her black True Religion jeans paired with a white t-shirt and all black Jordans was in stark contrast to the usually dressy Kayla.

"Where you going this early?" *Damn, I almost made it.*

"Class," Kayla answered as she turned around and gave him a passionate kiss on the lips.

"I hope you can be late."

Terry began to unbuckle Kayla's recently buttoned jeans as she protested about having to get to class. Seeing that her fight was futile, she let Terry undress her and pull her onto her bed. Before Kayla knew it, she was moaning and digging her nails in his back, forgetting all about her haste to make it to class.

When Kayla finally glanced at the clock, after what felt like hours, she knew that she would not be attending class. Instead, she decided she wanted to show Terry around Baton Rouge, (even though there was not much to see), and maybe go to a late movie. But, at that particular moment, she was content just lying in his arms as he drifted back off to sleep. *Just like a nigga to get some, and then fall asleep.* As Kayla snuggled closer under him, she smirked as she thought, *I wonder if we have some ice cream.*

Kayla awoke to Terry gently shaking her.

"Baby, I have to get back to the H. There is some shit I have to handle."

Kayla eyes snapped open as she sat up. "But I am not ready for you to go. You just got here."

"Kayla, I will pick you up from the airport Friday. I will call you when I make it back to Houston."

Kayla wouldn't kiss Terry back as he tried to kiss her before he left. *Why does he have to leave? He just got here. Whatever it is can wait.* Ignoring Kayla's attitude, Terry signaled to Chris, and they both headed out the door. As soon as Kayla heard the front door slam, she put her face in her pillow and sobbed silently to herself. Lately, she had been crying a lot, and in the back of her head, she wondered when she had become so damn emotional.

****

On the flight back to Houston, Terry couldn't stop thinking about Kayla. He didn't want to leave her, but duty had called. Terry had just got word that one of his best soldiers had got popped by narcotics, and he needed to get back to Houston to find out what had happened. The reason why Terry was able to stay in power was because he stayed on top of his business. Terry was good to those that were loyal to him, but crossing him meant the ultimate penalty.

Terry was not the only one who made out well from his lucrative illegal operation, and though he made sure his workers were taken care of, anyone in the streets knew that crossing Terry meant immediate death. In the world Terry lived in, there was no such thing as innocent until proven guilty. Snitching meant death, and his soldier had better hope that he kept his mouth shut till Terry could get Spicks, his lawyer, to the precinct. Terry was not sure Kayla was ready for this part of him, and he knew that things would be a lot less complicated if she left him alone.

****

As Kayla lay on the couch with a large bowl of butter pecan ice cream and her head in Pharris's lap, she couldn't help but think about the way her life was headed. She was falling for someone she knew nothing about, and, besides that, he made her body and heart tremble in ways that she didn't know they could. It had been almost seven hours since Terry had left, and she had yet to receive a phone call. As she ate her ice cream, both of her roommates tried to cheer her from her solemn mood, but nothing was working.

"Have you heard from Chris, Jordan?" Kayla asked as she looked over to where Jordan was sitting with a hopeful expression on her face.

"Nope," Jordan answered as she flipped through the channels on their sixty inch plasma TV.

Kayla lay her head back down in defeat as Pharris brushed her hair like a parent would a sulking child.

"He's going to call. Just be patient, Kayla," Pharris said with her usual optimism.

Kayla ignored her as she dialed Terry's cell phone number for the tenth time in the last hour. His phone went straight to voicemail. *Maybe he's with someone else...*Kayla tried to erase the visions of Terry making love to a mystery woman as tears again began to gather in her eyes. Dareon had messed her head all up. She didn't have any reason whatsoever to think that Terry was messing with someone else, but, here she was, already jumping to conclusions. Just then, her phone began to vibrate like crazy....Dareon.....*Damn, just thinking his name made him call.* Kayla was neither in the mood, nor the mind frame to speak to Dareon, so she sent him straight to voicemail. Again, her phone began to vibrate.

"Stop fuckin' calling me."

"Kayla, it's me. What's up with the attitude?"

Relieved to hear Terry's voice, Kayla decided to take the call and her ice cream into her bedroom.

"Why did it take you so long to call?"

"Kayla, I told you I had shit to handle. But I was just calling to let you know I hadn't forgotten about you. Let me hit you back later."

Kayla returned to the living room after Terry had abruptly ended what she thought would be a long conversation and assumed her position back on the couch.

"So, what did he say?" Jordan asked.

"That he is still handling his business," Kayla whimpered.

"Kayla, are you pregnant?" Jordan asked as she looked at Kayla from the corner of her eye. "Either you are pregnant or going through a midlife crisis because I know I have seen you cry, at least, twenty times this past week. And I know that's like your tenth bowl of ice cream. There is such a thing as being too emotional, but damn."

“No, I am not pregnant,” Kayla snapped as she tried to think back to her last period.

Now that she thought about, her period had been due almost a week ago, but maybe it was just late. Kayla, instantly, felt a headache coming on, because, if she was pregnant, she knew damn well it couldn’t be Terry’s.

The rest of the week passed by like a daze for Kayla, and still her period did not show. She had only talked to Terry twice since their last phone call, and she still was having a hard time sleeping since her attack. When Friday came, she double checked that her bag was packed and had Pharris drive her to the airport. Her mother had booked her flight out of Baton Rouge, instead of making her have to drive to New Orleans.

After checking in and passing through security, Kayla called Terry to make sure that he was still going to pick her up from the airport. His voicemail picked up immediately, so Kayla left a message. After the way he had been acting this week, she debated about calling her mother to pick her up, but decided to be patient. She could always call a taxi. And on top of feeling practically ignored by Terry, Dareon had been making it a point to call Kayla, at least, twelve times a day, ever since he realized she might be serious about leaving him alone this time. As Kayla sat in the airport and waited for her flight to be called, she couldn’t fight the urge to buy a pint of butter pecan ice cream from the creamery in the terminal.

****

Kayla landed in Houston at around four P.M. She couldn’t decide whether it was the flight or ice cream that had her queasy, but she couldn’t wait to get to her parents’ home. After collecting her rolling bag from the baggage claim area, she went out front to look for Terry. To her amazement, he was parked up front and seemed to be arguing with security about moving his vehicle from the loading zone. As she walked up, she saw Terry point her out to the security guard, who walked off with a scowl on his face. Terry hopped out of his truck and loaded Kayla's luggage into the back as she got into the passenger side. Once Terry had secured the hatch on the back of his vehicle, he eased back behind the wheel and into the outgoing airport traffic.

"How was your flight?"

"It was okay. I tried to call you before I left the airport. Why was your phone off?"

"Business, but I did get your message, though."

"It's always business with you."

Terry ignored Kayla's last comment as he scanned through the satellite radio stations to find a suitable song. He, finally, stopped on Robin Thicke's "Lost Without You". As soon as Kayla heard the song, she immediately changed the station. It used to be her and Dareon's song, and she did not want to hear it ever again, let alone with Terry.

"What's up with you? I like that song." Terry changed the station back.

"Well, I don't," Kayla said as she changed the station again.

"Don't ever touch a black man's radio," Terry said as they went back and forth changing the stations.

Kayla was not satisfied until she heard the song finally coming to an end. Eager to wipe the smirk off of Kayla's face, Terry ejected the face from his custom radio, immediately engulfing the car in silence. If he couldn't hear what he wanted, they would just have to ride the rest of the way in silence.

"Put it back," Kayla pouted as she tried to reach over him and attempt to reassemble the radio, but Terry would not relent.

Kayla finally gave in after seeing that she could not win, and began to try to annoy the hell out of Terry by singing an off-tune rendition of "Understanding" by SWV. Terry just ignored her, pissing her off even more, as he headed down I-10.

Their first stop was by Kayla's mother's home, west of Houston, in a gated community known as Weston Lakes. As Kayla approached the gate, a sense of nervousness overtook her. How was her mother going to react to meeting Terry for the first time? Terry was so different from any other guy she had ever brought home, and with his tattoo on his neck bearing another female's name, she was not sure how her mother was going to take her new beau. As the large gate eased open, allowing them access into her posh neighborhood, Kayla put on a smile and hoped for the best.

Kayla directed Terry through the neighborhood and into her driveway. Although her home was nowhere near as expansive as Dareon's, it still was rather impressive. A five bedroom, four and a half bath home built on a custom one acre golf course with a sparkling pool, spa, and waterfall with a lazy river. This was the home that Kayla had lived in all of her life. As she stuck her key in the lock and opened the set of double doors to enter her home, her miniature Yorkey, Gumdrop, ran up to meet them. She scooped him up in her arms and led Terry into the kitchen where she was sure to find her mother. At this time of the day, Mrs. Davis was sure to be preparing dinner, as she had done at nearly the same time every day for the past twenty something odd years.

"Hi, Mom!"

Kayla was right on the money. She put down a barking Gumdrop and kissed her mother on the cheek. She had missed her parents.

"This is Terry."

"Hi, Terry."

Mrs. Davis stirred her stew one last time, and then, to Kayla's surprise, Mrs. Davis embraced Terry with a warm hug. Mrs. Davis didn't know what type of relationship Terry and Kayla shared, but she liked the glow emanating from her daughter. She could tell Terry's character might be somewhat different than what she was used to, but she would have to learn to overlook that for now, at least, for her daughter's sake.

Kayla and Terry took adjoining seats at two of the bar stools that surrounded the marble topped kitchen island and quickly became engulfed in conversation with her mother. As her mother cooked, the trio talked about everything from Houston weather to LSU football, trying their best to not bring up Kayla's unfortunate attack. There was a time and place for that conversation, and, unbeknownst to Kayla, Ms. Davis had scheduled a counseling session for her beginning the following Monday in Baton Rouge.

"Hi, baby! Who's your guest?" Kayla's father greeted the group as he came in from an afternoon of golf on his private course, his favorite weekend pastime.

"Daddy, this is Terry," Kayla said, introducing the two as she gave her dad a kiss on the cheek. Nothing made her happier than coming home and seeing her parents together, because it didn't seem that long ago she was still trying to cope with their divorce.

"Mom, do you have any ice cream?" Kayla asked as she explored the freezer.

"Ice cream? You know in this house you will eat dinner before ice cream, Kayla Nicole Davis," Mrs. Davis chastised, causing Terry to smirk. *At least somebody knows how to keep Kayla's spoiled ass in place.*

It turned out the stew was Kayla's favorite, vegetable soup. To Kayla's dismay, Terry had to leave before dinner to go and wrap up some loose ends with his "business". She had just about had it with all this business shit.

"So, what type of work does Terry do?" Kayla's father asked over dinner.

"He owns his own business," Kayla answered while trying to steering the conversation elsewhere. But her inquisitive father was unrelenting.

"What type of business?"

"This and that."

"What does that mean, Kayla?"

Fed up with all this questioning about Terry, Kayla answered, "He was here. Why didn't you ask him?"

"Kayla, don't speak to your father in that tone. As your parents, we have a right to ask our daughter about the young man she decided to bring into our home. Now, answer your father." Kayla's mother spoke harshly as she glared in Kayla's direction.

She was no fool, and Kayla's desire to avoid the questioning, only enhanced her suspicions of what Terry did for a living. Mrs. Davis had been a lawyer for going on twenty-five years, and she knew a dope dealer when she saw one.

Instead of answering her mother, Kayla proceeded to eat her meal in silence. Both her parents just let her be, sensing that the conversation was not going to go anywhere. They both knew that their daughter was as stubborn as a mule.

After dinner, Kayla helped her mother clean the kitchen. Although Kayla's mother had let her slide during dinner with the conversation about Terry, Kayla knew that, once her dad left, it would be a different story.

"Kayla, Terry is into illegal activities, isn't he?

"I don't know."

"Kayla, as the Lord is my witness, if you don't answer me, so help me God."

"Mom, if you already know, then why are you asking?"

"Because you are my only child and I will ask whatever I want, whenever I damn well please."

Kayla dried the dishes in silence as she listened to her mother rant and rave about the dangers of dating someone that was into illegal business. As far as she was concerned, all of that was irrelevant. She was falling hard for Terry, and that was all that mattered. *Maybe I can convince him to leave the game.* She figured that he had to have a lot of money stacked away, and maybe she was what he needed to get his life in order.

After thoroughly cleaning the kitchen and putting up the leftover food, Kayla's mother retreated into her master bedroom to prepare for bed. Kayla's mother was the exact opposite of her daughter. She was an early riser and usually was sound asleep before 9:30. All throughout high school, Kayla's mother's sleeping habits had allowed Kayla to roam the streets at her free will, as long as she made it back home before her mother woke up around seven A.M.

Kayla retreated into her childhood bedroom that had changed very little since high school. The room was still covered in WordUp posters, baring pictures of her adolescent crushes like Ginuwine and Usher. She smiled to herself as she recalled the countless times she had argued her friends up and down that, when she grew up, she was going to be a background dancer for Usher and make him fall in love with her. As Kayla laid back on her oversized canopy bed, she retrieved her cell and called Terry.

"What are you doing?"

"On my way to get you."

"Why didn't you call first?"

"Because I knew you would call first. Just be ready. I will be there in fifteen minutes."

****

"Police are investigating the homicide of a man recently indicted for attacking a female LSU student this past Sunday in the home of football star, Dareon Anderson. Julian Michum, 32, was found with multiple gunshot wounds in his home in Dallas, Texas. At this time, police are not sure whether there is a connection between the attack and his murder."

Nicole paced her living room, half listening to the news coverage. Her head throbbed as she gently rubbed her temples. There was just too much going on, and she felt like she was losing control. Samara was still planning on having Dareon's baby, and this shit with Kayla had gone too far. Her contacts in Houston had told her that Kayla was in Houston with Terry at this very moment. How were her family and her peers going to react when Dareon showed up at the next reunion with a bastard child, and his cousin showed up with Dareon's ex girlfriend? And, on top of that, the foolproof plan that she had concocted with Julian, her gardener's son, had backfired in her face. *Good thing somebody got to him before I did.*

Julian had been paid a handsome fee to rough Kayla up and warn her about messing with Terry, but her heroic son had saved the day. The bruises that Kayla received were minimal, considering the price she had paid.

As Nicole sat on the sofa, she reached into her purse to retrieve two valiums and her cell phone. Maybe she couldn't do anything about Samara for the moment, but she wondered how Kayla's parents would feel if they knew their daughter was dating one of the biggest drug dealers in the South. And it was past time that she made a trip to Baton Rouge to help her son clean up his messes.

****

Kayla giggled as she sipped Moet in Terry's oversized Jacuzzi while he tickled her feet. She knew what type of life Terry lived, but—Damn!—she had no idea that he was doing it this big. Terry stayed in a newer subdivision in Katy, TX on the outskirts of Houston. Surprisingly, his home was located less than fifteen minutes from her parents. Terry's five bedroom, seven bathroom home came equipped with a lake view from almost every angle of the house, a master bedroom with four large walk-in closets, a private patio, an executive style garden tub in the master bathroom with marble steps and a shower big enough for six people, and, in the backyard, there was an oversized deck with a hot tub to die for. The hot tub was surrounded by lush foliage, which was rare for this time of year, and it was encrusted in marble and twenty-four karat gold accents.

Terry's home was also equipped with a state of the art security system that captured every angle of the home and was monitored around the clock by a few of his most trusted men. And, as an added security measure, patrolling the grounds of the property 24/7 were four fierce Dobermans that only Terry, Chris, and Shon could control. They had been trained to attack at even the smallest threat. Terry took his business seriously, and did not believe in ever having to serve any jail time.

His product was never brought into his home, and he made sure that he moved his storage locations so frequently that even the most seasoned detective would not be able to catch on. For the most part, any investigator or government official who was not on his payroll, knew that trying to catch Terrence Jaylen Carver would cost more time and resources than they had to invest.

"Terry, stop! I hate being tickled," Kayla giggled.

Terry continued to tickle Kayla until she was panting.

"Stop," she pleaded and tried to catch her breath.

He took her drink from her hand and began planting kisses on her neck and down her chest. Even in the slightly cool air, Kayla knew it was Terry's lips that were causing the chills to cascade down her spine. She felt Terry reach behind her neck, and undo the strings that held together her skimpy Armani bikini.

As she felt him gently removing her top, she pushed his head down to her breasts, sighing as he licked and sucked on each of her nipples lovingly. *Damn, I want to feel his tongue below my waist.* As if he'd read her mind, Terry lifted Kayla onto the edge of the Jacuzzi and removed her bikini bottom in one swift motion. As he held her hips, he eased his tongue inside of her, and lightly sucked and prodded until he found her clit.

Once he found her clit, he alternated between using his fingers and his tongue to make her reach her first climax. Not satisfied until he was, Kayla slid back into the water, took a long breath of air and slid underneath. Freeing Terry's dick from his shorts, she bopped underneath as she deep throated all eight inches of him, while he watched from above. When Kayla couldn't hold her breath anymore, she broke surface and kissed Terry with all the passion she could muster. Not needing any further initiative, Terry spread Kayla's legs and entered her forcefully. She held onto his neck, while he entered her over and over, even the bubbling and gushing of the Jacuzzi water could not drown out their moans.

When they finally exited the Jacuzzi, they were both exhausted. Wrapped in towels, they entered the house and walked through the marble-tiled living room and up the winding staircase into Terry's master bedroom. Kayla spread out nude on the black one thousand thread count sheets and matching comforter, and opened her arms for Terry to join her. It seemed that, no matter how exhausted she was, she would never get tired of making love to Terry.

And it seemed that, no matter how many times they made each other climax, they could still go over and over again with barely a rest in between. Unwilling to let Kayla down, Terry climbed in bed, on top of her, to finish what had been started in the Jacuzzi. Kayla wrapped her legs around Terry's back, as he again pleased her in ways that her body had never known. She had always heard there was a difference between fucking a boy and a man, and, as Terry made her scream his name over and over again, she knew that the rumors were true. Terry was a bonafide man, and, each and every time he made her climax, Dareon was pushed further into the back of her mind.

****

Dareon lay back on his bed with his head propped on several pillows as he watched Samara ride his dick. He had heard that pregnant pussy was the best pussy, but this was pure ecstasy. Just when he felt himself about to cum, he held her down as he shot his entire load into her already pregnant walls. At least with Samara, he could fuck her without a condom, because, as much as she harassed the hell out of him, he knew that she wasn't fucking anyone else, and, shit, the bitch was already knocked up.

The first thing Dareon's mother had done when Samara started claiming that she was pregnant was pay for Samara to go to a well-known gynecologist in Baton Rouge to verify that she was actually pregnant and to test her for any STDs. But as hard as Dareon had prayed, while the STD test had come back negative, the pregnancy test had definitely come back positive.

Dareon moved Samara from his now soft dick and got up to go into the restroom, taking his cell phone with him. *Where the hell is Kayla, and why is she still not answering my calls? She can't be taking Terry seriously, can she?* As he let the shower water engulf him, he dialed Kayla's number. *This is Kayla. Leave a message...*The phone went to voicemail after two rings, indicating that Kayla had sent him to voicemail…again.

Samara lay in the bed, naked, and ran her hands over her slowly rounding belly. *Why in the hell is Dareon taking his cell phone into the shower, and why doesn't he ever invite me to join him?* She couldn't understand why Dareon couldn't just love her the way that he loved that stuck-up bitch Kayla, and support her decision to keep their baby. She knew she loved him, and had since the first time she had seen him. Part of the reason she had decided to sleep with him so soon was because she knew in her heart that Dareon was her soul mate. *Why can't Dareon see that we are meant to be?*

It was like he didn't even acknowledge her unless he was looking for a quick nut or trying to talk her into having an abortion, which she was not going to do under any circumstances. The only part of Dareon that she had was this baby, and not even $20,000 would make her get rid of that. He would love her one day. He would have to, especially after she had his baby.

****

To the dismay of Kayla's parents, Kayla spent the entire weekend at Terry's house, less the one meal she had eaten at home when she first arrived. As Kayla kissed her parents goodbye and Terry waited in his truck to take her back to the airport, she had to listen to her mother's bitter complaining about not putting any male before her family. This was not how she had expected this good-bye to go, and had she known her mother was waiting to fuss, she would have called her parents from her cell phone instead. But being the good daughter that she tried to be, she sucked up her mother's lecture with a smile, and waited patiently until she finished. Sensing her daughter's anxiety to leave, Mr. and Mrs. Davis kissed Kayla on each of her cheeks and bid her farewell as they waved to Terry. Some lessons Kayla would just have to learn on her own.

As soon as Kayla was out of sight, Mrs. Davis walked to the end of the driveway to check the mail. As she pulled out what seemed like an endless amount of envelopes, her eyes fell on a manila envelope that was blank except for her name printed in large black letters. Someone had obviously dropped this package off at her house, and, as curiosity got the best of her, she opened the sealed envelope as she walked back up the driveway.

Chapter 14

"Terry, are you ignoring me for like the fifth time?" Kajuana snapped as she rolled her eyes. For the past month, it seemed like he was either always busy or daydreaming the couple of times he had made time for her.

"I'm just chillin'. Damn," Terry muttered, not even trying to mask his irritation.

Kajuana had only been in his vehicle for a few minutes, but he was already ready to put her nagging ass out. Last that he checked, she was not his girlfriend, and never would be.

"You know what, Terry? Lashon's cousin's baby mama, CiCi, told me she saw you at Ladonna's house last week. I know that ghetto ho's not the reason you acting all funny and stuff," Kajuana fussed as she batted her long, fake eyelashes and tapped her lime green nails against the door panel.

"I'm taking you back home," Terry replied as he made an illegal U-turn and headed back the way he had just come.

"Whatever, nigga," Kajuana fumed as she patted her multi-colored tracks and rolled her eyes. "You'll be back, as soon as you realize that I am a dime piece that you can't live without."

Terry almost laughed out loud as he compared Kajuana to Kayla. There was just simply no comparison. Hands down, Kayla was everything that Kajuana thought she was. As he thought about Kayla's perfect smile and their conversations, a tiny smirk erupted on his face.

"What is so damn funny?" Kajuana asked looking Terry up and down.

"Just happy to be dropping your ass off," Terry responded as he pulled his truck to a stop in front of her Section 8 apartment.

For months, Kajuana had broken Terry off any way that he wanted. But now it was like he didn't want anything to do with her. Every time she called, he blew her off, and getting him to spend time with her was like pulling teeth. And ever since he had got back from South Padre, sex had been out the question. He hadn't even let her give him the head that he used to be so fond of. As Kajuana exited the vehicle, she made sure to slam the door so hard that the windows around her rattled.

Not even fazed, Terry screeched off. She wasn't the first female that he had let go in the couple of months that he'd been messing with Kayla, and she wouldn't be the last. And even though he hadn't seen Kayla at all in the weeks since she left Houston, he had managed to keep his dick in his pants. Sex alone was no longer enough to satisfy his needs, and he craved the feeling of Kayla's naked body against his afterward. The other females could no longer compare. As he eased back onto the interstate and to his residence in Katy, he activated his Bluetooth and called Kayla.

Back in her apartment, Kajuana stripped out of her Baby Phat Gear and stalked around her apartment naked. She'd had her night all planned out, and Terry had spoiled it, as he'd had a tendency of doing lately. First, they were going to go out to eat, then to a movie, and then she had planned to talk Terry into taking her back to his place. As she paced her living room, she tried to think of the last time she had been to his place. *He must be messing with someone else.* Refusing to let Terry get the best of her, she retrieved her cell and dialed a number by memory.

"Hello. Who dis?"

"Kajuana."

"Where my nigga Terry?"

"We through."

"Sure you are. He must not be fucking with you tonight."

"What fuckin' ever, Shon. You coming or not?"

"Be there in an hour. Just let me kiss the wife and kids goodnight. And get the ice ready, you know how I fuckin' like it."

****

Kayla sighed as she turned past the well-manicured lawn and into the set of office suites that looked like small homes. Her mother had first made her an appointment with a Mrs. Deverie weeks ago, and after several reschedules, she was finally following her mother's orders.

She hated counseling sessions and had only endured them to overcome her parents' divorce because, at that particular time, she really missed having her mother in her life. And plus, she had heard from the arresting officer of her case that her attacker had been found dead in his apartment. She shuddered at the thought that Terry had something to do with his murder, but there were some things she would rather not know. Finally mustering her nerve, Kayla turned off her car and walked to the building with a sign out front that read THERAPY BY DEVERIE. *Oh, great! Signify to the world that I need help.*

Kayla entered the neatly decorated building and was greeted by an overly chipper secretary, "Good morning. May I have your name please?"

"Kayla Davis."

"Well, have a seat. Mrs. Deverie will be with you shortly."

Kayla took the nearest seat to the door and turned her phone on vibrate. Before she put her phone away, she decided to send Terry a text: I think I'm falling hard.

"Kayla?" A petite brown skinned woman with a full head of silver hair signaled Kayla to follow her to a back room. Since Kayla had been to counseling before, she was surprised by the décor of this room; it was unlike the stiff rooms where she had previously had therapy. This room was decorated with bright colors, shades of turquoise, yellow, and orange, and, instead of the drab couch that Kayla was expecting, in the center of the room, next to a large window, was a plush looking red Italian leather sofa covered in a variety of colorful pillows. The view outside of the window was a large picturesque lake with a waterfall in the middle and a variety of ducks either walking on the bank or swimming in the distance. Instead of being signaled over to the couch, Kayla was instructed to sit in one of the oversized armchairs in front of Mrs. Deverie's desk.

"So, what brings you here today?" Mrs. Deverie asked Kayla as she adjusted her glasses on the tip of her nose and gave Kayla her full attention.

Unsure of what to say, Kayla began by telling Mrs. Deverie about the attack in as much detail as she could remember. As she spoke, she was surprised that Mrs. Deverie seemed to be listening intently. *Isn't she supposed to be writing notes or something?*

"So, is Dareon your boyfriend?" Mrs. Deverie asked, staring at Kayla over the rims of her glasses.

"Well, he was…" Kayla tried to choose her words carefully. *How do I say he was, but I am now dating his cousin?*

"Please continue, Kayla."

"I am now fooling around with his cousin."

Kayla let her last sentence out in one big gush, not anticipating the questions that she was sure to follow. Instead, Mrs. Deverie looked at her watch and announced that their one hour session was over. She handed Kayla a prescription for a valium to help her sleep at night, and made an appointment for the following Monday. Kayla left the office feeling better than when she had first came in, and even though she had not gotten a chance to divulge her drama filled life to Mrs. Deverie, she knew that the time would soon come when Mrs. Deverie would know all too much about Kayla Nicole Davis.

When Kayla got back into her car, she pulled out her cell, secretly anticipating a message or phone call from Terry. She, instead, had six missed calls from her mother and a voicemail. Not sure what was so urgent, she quickly dialed her mother back, and prayed that nothing had happened to her father.

"Kayla, I am on my way to Baton Rouge as we speak."

"Why? What's wrong?" Kayla asked as she sat with her hand perched on the steering wheel, unable to put the car into reverse until she knew what was wrong.

"Someone just sent me pictures of Terry, and some of the pictures include you in some very compromising positions." Mrs. Davis paused before continuing, the images of her only child and Terry in the hot tub forever implanted in her mind. "I want you to see these pictures, and see what a disgrace you are causing your family. Pick me up at the airport at three." Mrs. Davis disconnected.

Kayla could feel her hands shaking as she rested her head on the steering wheel. *Who would do such a sick, heartless thing?* Her mother knew she was no virgin, especially after she got pregnant in high school, but, for someone to send pictures of her making love to Terry, that was just too much. Kayla could feel hot tears running down her face, but more than sadness, she felt anger for whoever could do such a thing. She threw her car into reverse and headed to Dareon's house. She could not think of anyone who had a better motive than her asshole of an ex-boyfriend.

As she pulled into his parking garage, she could not mistake Dareon and Samara standing in front of his truck engaged in what seemed to be a heated conversation. Not wanting to interrupt the two love birds, Kayla waited until she saw Samara hop in Dareon's truck and speed off. *Oh, so he does let hos drive his truck.*

As soon as Kayla saw Dareon's truck turn onto the main street, she eased out of her car and confronted Dareon as he walked towards the elevator.

"It's good to know just how low you can stoop, Dareon."

"What the fuck are you talking about, Kayla? I just let her use my truck to get her crazy ass out of my face. I know you have been getting my calls."

"I don't give a damn about which bitch you let drive your truck, Dareon. In case you forgot, we are done." Kayla paused to let her words sink in. "But why in the fuck did you send pictures of me and Terry to my mom?" It took everything in Kayla not to slap Dareon as the reality of her words sunk in. Not sure how detailed the pictures were, she could imagine the hurt in her mother's eyes as she watched Terry fuck her daughter in every possible position.

"I don't know what you are talking about, Kayla," Dareon said as they both got on the elevator that led to his condo.

"Who else would do some shit like that?"

"I don't know, Kayla, but I promise I didn't do it."

As they entered the condo, Dareon kneeled down on one knee in front of Kayla.

"Kayla, I promise I didn't do that shit, but I miss the hell out of you. I know I fucked up, but please take me back."

"I don't want anything to do with you." Kayla turned to leave his condominium, realizing that he was not about to admit to what he had done. But Dareon refused to let her go, grabbing her by her waist.

"Let me go, Dareon, or I will scream."

"I don't care, Kayla. I love you, and you are not even trying to make this work."

"Dareon, where were you when I was trying for three years to make it work? Where were you when I was crying every night? I don't need you in my life, nor do I want you. I hate you, and I would rather fuck Terry than your nasty ass any day."

Hearing those words, Dareon reached back and slapped Kayla before he realized what he was doing. As soon as his hand left her cheek and he watched her fall to the floor, pity filled him fast as lightning. "Kayla, I am so sorry."

Kayla recoiled as he reached out to touch her, and, for once, he did not try and stop her as she wildly swung blows at him.

"How could you hit me? I fuckin' hate you! I fuckin' hate you!" Kayla screamed as she hit Dareon over and over again.

Dareon let Kayla hit him over and over again until she was out of breath from both fighting him and crying at the same time. He lifted her tired frame into his arms and carried her into his bedroom.

As tears cascaded down both of their faces, Dareon knew that, this time, his tears were genuine. He missed the hell out of his girlfriend. When they reached the bedroom, Kayla was too tired to continue fighting. She allowed

Dareon to rock her like a baby and apologize repeatedly for letting his anger get the best of him. Before Kayla knew it, his words had turned into kisses, and he was unbuttoning her blouse.

"Dareon, please stop. I can't do this. I want Terry..."

Kayla begged but Dareon ignored her cries while undressing her. Whether or not she knew it, each and every time Kayla mentioned Terry's name, it made him want to make love to Kayla even more, just so that she would know she would always be his.

Weakened from her tears, and even weaker from Dareon's kisses, Kayla felt her body betraying her and succumbing to Dareon's whims. By the time Dareon got under her clothes to remove her panties, Kayla was in his total control. Dareon laid Kayla on the bed, and immediately went below to taste Kayla. Oh, how he missed the taste of her.

As he licked and sucked below, Kayla held his head down and moaned out his name. Still in disbelief at what she was doing, she was, by this time, too far gone to stop what was already in progress. After Dareon made Kayla cum, he entered her.

Savoring the moment, Dareon rode Kayla, slowly surprised at how snug his dick still fit considering...He flipped Kayla onto her stomach and entered her from behind as they moaned in pleasure. No matter how bad Kayla wanted to stop, she could not control herself as she threw it back to match his pace. As Dareon entered Kayla as deep as her walls would allow, he couldn't help but think that his cousin was hitting it the same way. As Dareon picked up speed, Kayla grimaced in both pain and pleasure. He asked Kayla over and over again whose it was and did not climax until Kayla screamed out his name as she came all over his freshly laundered sheets.

Realizing what she had done almost as soon as she exhaled from her second orgasm, Kayla rolled out from under Dareon's weight. Ashamed, she dressed quickly and ran out of Dareon's apartment.

As she sat in her car and tried to gather her composure, she noticed the indicator light flashing on her cell phone. New message from Terry…Kayla opened the message and hated herself immediately: Me too, Kay, but I can't figure out if it's your beauty or your booty though. You need to come down here, so I can figure it out."

****

Dareon lay on his bed with a smirk on his face. He had not sent the pictures, but thank God to whoever had, because they had allowed Kayla to fall right into his trap. Naked, he sauntered over to his closet and stepped in front of the red flashing light carefully concealed behind several hats. As he stopped his video camera and removed the tape, he couldn't help but gloat secretly to himself. No matter how much Kayla resented him, she still had a weakness for him in her heart. And after Dareon made sure that Terry saw just how much she missed him, she would have no choice but to come crawling back on begging knees.

Chapter 15

Terry and Chris rolled through their old hood in Terry's Denali, peeping the scene. Every so often they had to make an appearance to make sure that business was getting handled and, sometimes, to set an example or two. They hadn't made racks by sitting in the house, allowing other people to control their business. The game had been going in their favor for far too long, and the plan was to keep it that way.

"So, I'm really feeling Kayla."

Chris was shocked by Terry's admission and remained silent to let him continue to talk.

"Loyalty is everything to me, but I think I am going to have to go ahead and talk to Dareon like a man. I haven't felt like this about anyone, since Samantha, and you know that's been a minute."

"Well, you definitely are going to have to have that talk with Dareon. Low key, you might have to put a bullet between that nigga's eyes. I'm just saying. Be glad y'all niggas are family."

****

After Kayla left Dareon's place, she headed straight to the neighborhood CVS Pharmacy. Jordan's words were in her head as she headed down the aisle that contained pregnancy tests. *Could I really be pregnant?* Her period was long overdue, and no matter how she tried to ignore all the symptoms, from slight nausea in the morning to her craving for ice cream and her compulsive mood swings, which included crying at the slightest things, Kayla knew she was pregnant. She bought two tests just to be sure, and, when she got home and saw the pink lines on both, her worst fear was confirmed. Not only was she pregnant, but she seriously doubted the baby could be Terry's. By the time that she had slept with Terry in South Padre, her period had already been late. For what seemed like the hundredth time that day, Kayla threw herself on her bed and burst into tears.

At three o'clock sharp, Kayla was at the airport to pick up her mother. It seemed like her symptoms had intensified since she found out she was pregnant, because, as she waited, she couldn't help guzzling down a pint of butter pecan ice cream. Kayla saw her mother first, and, as she pulled into the loading zone, she concealed the now empty ice cream container and any other evidence of her feast in a plastic bag and pushed it under her seat. Kayla didn't want to take any chances of her mother finding out she was pregnant, at least, not until she figured out what she was going to do. And with all the current drama going on, she knew that this was the last thing she wanted to concern her mother with. Kayla would leave the situation alone until her mother left, but, sooner or later, she and Dareon would have to talk about their very big problem. *It isn't like this would be his first time having the "I might be your baby mama" conversation.*

As Kayla watched her mother walk to the car, she couldn't help but notice the very large manila envelope her mother had clutched in her hand.

"Kayla, let me drive." Instead of a hello or how are you, Kayla was greeted with the envelope being practically thrown into her lap. "Look at that, and tell me if you are proud of what you see. Kayla, I am so ashamed of you right now."

Kayla opened the envelope and gasped at the images that she saw. Not only were there pictures of her and Terry in the hot tub, there were also pictures of Kayla and Terry at his house in South Padre. Kayla felt as if she couldn't breath as she flipped through picture after picture. Each one seemed worse than the last. Someone had to really hate Kayla to send this type of stuff to her mother.

"Has Dad seen these?" Kayla asked as she continued to stare at the photos, too ashamed to even look at her mother.

"No, I didn't want to kill him."

Kayla glanced at her mother from the corner of her eye. Mrs. Davis was looking at her with either pity or disgust. Kayla couldn't tell which one from this angle.

The ride back to Kayla's apartment was silent, except for the swish of the windshield wipers to combat the light drizzle that had started on the way from the airport. As soon as they pulled into Kayla's parking garage, Mrs. Davis asked her to carry up her bag, while she went to run a very important errand. Unsure of what type of errand she had in Baton Rouge, Kayla just obeyed and carried the overnight bag to her apartment. Once in her room, Kayla climbed beneath her covers and made herself go to sleep.

****

Mrs. Davis pulled up in front of the Hilton in downtown Baton Rouge a little before four P.M. She had received a phone call from Dareon's mother to meet her there, and she could tell by the tone on the other end that this was one meeting she did not need to miss. As Mrs. Davis gave her keys to the valet, she adjusted the jacket of her Prada business suit and headed to the restaurant area to meet Dareon's mom, whom she was sure had made reservations.

Picking out Dareon's mom immediately, the only black woman in this section of the establishment, Mrs. Davis waved off the hostess as she made a beeline straight for Nicole Anderson's table. She could tell by the stern look on the face of this very unattractive woman that this meeting would be all business, and that was fine with her, because her main concern was protecting her daughter. Not one to be intimidated, Mrs. Davis took a seat adjacent to Nicole and applied her all business face. As a well-known lawyer in Houston with a reputation that preceded her, she knew to be ready to expect anything from this rigid rich bitch.

"Mrs. Anderson, since this meeting was so urgent, what exactly is the nature of your request for me to meet you here?"

"A woman who gets down to business. I like that. And please call me Nicole," she said as she took a sip from her glass of top shelf Merlot. "Do you want anything to drink? It's on me," Mrs. Anderson waved a nearby waitress over to their table.

"A glass of cognac please," Mrs. Davis ordered, sure that her choice of drink was unimpressive to this member of fine society.

She knew she would need a stiff drink to get through this luncheon, because, after putting two and two together, it didn't take a rocket scientist to figure out who had sent the pictures to her. The pictures had been the last of two deliveries to her home. While the first one had contained Terry's juvenile records, which were no surprise, the second package had been the one that had threw her into a rage. Any woman who would stoop that low clearly had a dangerous motive, and the motive was what Mrs. Davis was here to find out more about.

"I am sure you are eager to find out why I requested this meeting," Nicole said, toying with Mrs. Davis, who she could tell was eager to be anywhere but there. "And I assume you got the package I sent you."

"I did. How tasteless of you, Nicole."

Ignoring the last part of Mrs. Davis's comment, Nicole continued. "I am sure you know that your daughter broke up with my son and is now screwing his cousin, Terry. Excuse me for saying this, but that is rather tasteless, don't you think?" Not waiting for an answer, Nicole again continued as Kayla's mother sat nursing her cognac carefully. "Now, I don't like for my son to be hurt, as no parent does, and I think that we would both benefit if your daughter left Terry alone."

"Well, excuse me for saying, but I think that my daughter should be allowed to date whomever she damn well pleases."

"Screwing and dating are definitely two different things. But I figured you would need a bit more persuading, so just to let you know there are a lot more of those pictures to pass around. And I don't think that your little lawyer friends would view your little family the same if they knew your daughter was dating a dope dealer."

Kayla's mother downed the remainder of her drink and looked Mrs. Anderson right in the face.

"Bitch, let me tell you something. I don't know whether to pity you or kick your miserable ass, but my daughter is an adult and will date whomever she pleases. Now, as far as the pictures, do what you have to do because my family has overcome many obstacles greater than this one."

With that said, Mrs. Davis left a $20.00 bill on the table, which was more than enough to cover her drink and left.

As Dareon's mother sat at the table alone and nursed her third glass of merlot, she thought, *So, this bitch wants to play hardball.* Finishing off her glass, she retrieved her cellular phone from her purse.

"Have you talked to Terry yet?"

"Nope, I am on my way to meet him now."

"Who does he think that you are?"

"A new connect."

"Call me if the plan changes."

Mrs. Anderson powered off her cellular, and left a crisp $100.00 bill on the table in addition to Kayla's mother $20. As she headed back to her posh hotel suite, alarms chimed in her head as she contemplated her next move.

Kayla's mother pulled up to Kayla's apartment with a scowl on her face. As she tried to control the shaking in her hands, she bowed her head in prayer. *God give me the strength to get through this. My family needs you right now, and, with your strength, we will not allow this woman to destroy our family.* Gathering her composure, Mrs. Davis hit the alarm on Kayla's car and caught the elevator to her daughter's apartment. It was time that they had a long talk, and she, also, needed to tell Kayla that she had a flight scheduled to return to Houston later that night. Initially she was going to stay overnight, but, with all that was going on, she couldn't wait to get back to her husband.

As Mrs. Davis entered the apartment with Kayla's key, she was surprised at the silence. *Jordan and Pharris must be out,* Mrs. Davis thought as she headed into Kayla's room. Seeing Kayla sleeping, Mrs. Davis sat on the edge of Kayla's bed and stroked her hair.

"Where did you go, Mom?" Kayla asked yawning.

"Don't worry yourself, baby. I had to go and handle some business."

As Kayla's mother stroked her hair, the will to tell the truth overcame Kayla. She didn't know why she was unable to keep secrets from her mother and almost kicked herself when the words tumbled from her lips.

"Mom, I am pregnant."

Mrs. Davis continued stroking Kayla's hair, and, instead of acting irrationally, as Kayla had predicted, she handled it as best as could be expected.

"What are you going to do, Kayla, and have you told Terry?"

"I just found out, and, Mom," Kayla paused, "it's Dareon's baby."

Mrs. Davis slowly got up from Kayla's bed and walked over to the window. *Lord, please give me the strength. I know that you would never put more on any of us than we can bear, so I know that there is a meaning behind this.* Kayla's mother turned and faced her.

"Baby, we are going to make it through this. I know you have a lot going on right now, but all of this is just a test. The devil is just trying to discourage us. If you want to keep the baby, we have the means, and, if you choose not to, I will be there every step of the way.And we need to schedule you a doctor's appointment. It's a wonder you didn't miscarry after your brutal attack.

Kayla held out her arms to her mother who joined her in the bed. The two dozed off into a dreamless sleep, as they tried to cope with the trials that were ahead.

****

Terry, Chris, and Shon pulled up to a port in East Houston close to eleven P.M. They were meeting a new connect who was supposed to have some of the best product in the Southern states. The access to product in the states meant easier trafficking. The connect in Mexico had been alright at first, but two of their recent shipments had been confiscated by the feds.

As they pulled behind each other, each in separate cars, Terry used a prepaid phone to page the connect, whom he knew only by the name of S. Rogers, to notify them of their arrival. Within seconds of sending the page, a nearby warehouse opened up, signaling this was where the crew should enter. Feeling for his Glock, Terry led the way as the crew cautiously approached the warehouse entrance.

Terry had had the place cased before his arrival, and, just in case any shit went down, he had six of his best henchmen posted up at different spots surrounding the warehouse, keeping a close watch for any unwanted interferences.

As Terry entered the warehouse, he sensed that something was amiss. The warehouse was completely empty, except for a big screen television with a DVD hookup and a large throne. Shon and Chris drew their pieces and pointed them at the chair where they could see that someone was seated. As Terry circled the chair with his Glock in hand, ready to kill if necessary, his heart almost dropped when he saw who was seated in his presence.

Chapter 16

Kayla was awakened by her mother around eleven P.M., so she could be driven back to the airport. Neither had meant to sleep that late, but, with all that had gone on that day, it was almost inevitable. Kayla dropped her mom back off at the airport around 11:30, and then headed home. On her way, she dialed Terry. Unsurprisingly, she was greeted by his voicemail. This was getting old fast, and Kayla knew in her heart that, if something didn't change soon, she would have to allow him to become a figment of the past. What Kayla needed was someone who could be there for her. It seemed that every time she called Terry, he was always too busy handling his so-called business.

As Kayla approached her parking garage, the white Escalade parked in a visitor's spot did not go unnoticed. Too tired to fight Dareon at that particular moment, she parked her car and braced herself for the worst. Every time that she turned around, she was dealing with drama. Why should today be an exception? But to Kayla's surprise, perched near the elevator, with a tear-stained face, was Samara.

"To what do I owe the pleasure?" Kayla asked as she crossed her arms, displaying the attitude that she felt.

"Kayla, I didn't come here to start anything," Samara sniffled, "but there is something that you must know. I overheard Dareon and his mother talking, and they have something planned for Terry. I don't know what it is, but I know it's not anything good, and I have seen what Dareon's mother is capable of."

"And what turned you into the Good Samaritan?" Kayla asked, still unsure of whether she should believe Samara. All that Samara had ever brought into her life was a whole bunch of drama, and she could not figure out why she should trust her now.

"Kayla, I know this has nothing to do with you, but I just found out that Dareon's mother paid my doctor, whom she handpicked, to prescribe me an abortion pill, but to tell me that it was prenatal medicine. If I wouldn't have asked the pharmacist for additional instructions on the medication, she would have succeeded. This lady is capable of anything, and I just couldn't live with myself if something happened, and I did nothing to stop it."

Samara reached forward to retrieve a package from her purse and handed it to Kayla. Without another word, she hopped into Dareon's Escalade and roared out of the parking garage. As far as Samara was concerned, her good deed was done. Deciding to believe her, Kayla rushed to her car, and tried to call Terry. His phone went immediately to voicemail. Screeching her car into reverse, she plugged her cell phone into her car charger and headed towards I-10 to Houston. Kayla prayed as she gunned her car down the highway and thanked God she was on a full tank and wouldn't have to stop. She kept Terry's number on redial, determined to not stop calling until she heard from him. All thoughts except for Terry's wellbeing were put out of her mind as her car reached speeds exceeding 100 mph.

****

As Terry stared at the black beauty in front of him, feelings that he thought had been long suppressed re-emerged. *How could he be so stupid? S. Rogers? Samantha Rogers?* Terry lowered his pistol, not sure what to expect, and told his boys to do the same. She looked the same way she had looked the first day he had met her, not the coked out Samantha that he threw out and thought had overdosed. Smooth dark skin with silky black hair that cascaded down her back, and a body to die for, Samantha was here, alive, in the flesh. Sitting in the chair with one leg cocked over the side, revealing a smooth round thigh underneath her very short skirt, Samantha couldn't help but taunt Terry as she performed fellatio on a bright red lollipop.

"Is this how you greet the love of your life, Terrence?"

"I thought you were dead. What the fuck are you doing here? Is this some kind of sick joke?"

"I missed you, too, Terry." Samantha purred as she lifted her 5'3 frame from the large chair, adjusting the skirt that left nothing to the imagination.

Terry signaled for Chris and Shon to leave the room, slid his pistol back into his waistband, and closed the warehouse door. There was unfinished business in this room, and Terry planned to wrap it up and forever close this chapter in his life. At one point in his life, he couldn't see past Samantha, but shit had changed the day she killed their son.

Samantha signaled for Terry to sit in the seat she had just vacated. As Terry opened his mouth to protest, Samantha aggressively pushed him backwards, causing him to land in the chair. On reflex, Terry reached back to punch her, catching himself before he inflicted serious damage. Arm still raised, Terry hissed, "Bitch, don't ever put your hands on me again because, next time, I just might kill your ass. And this time, Chris won't be here to save you."

Laughing wickedly, Samantha walked over to the DVD player and hit the PLAY button. Not at all concerned with Terry's threat, she knew that, after he saw the footage that she had, he would be putty in her arms all over again. But this time around would be different, she was clean, thanks to his aunt, and, tonight, she planned to get her man back. When Terry threw her out, she had nowhere to go, and, on a whim, she showed up at his aunt's house in Dallas, where she and Nicole had connected many times before when Terry had brought her to family reunions and functions at the Anderson residence.

Nicole had secretly taken her in, without disputing the rumors that she had overdosed in the streets of Houston, and put her through an extensive rehab program. Samantha had been clean for over a year and was working for Ms. Nicole as her personal assistant, all the time waiting for the moment to resurrect herself to Terry, her only true love. Nicole's only requests of her until that time had been simple: stay clean and don't let anyone in the family know you're still alive.

When Nicole had come to her with the Kayla dilemma, Samantha knew that now was the time to get her man back and show Nicole her appreciation. Armed with the ammunition she held in the DVD player, nothing would stand in her way of gaining access back into Terry's heart.

Samantha stood back and watched Terry's expression as he watched the film begin to play. She watched as his jaw clenched tight as he watched Dareon fuck Kayla and listened to Kayla moaning in ecstacy as she fucked Dareon back. Terry couldn't control the anger creeping into his emotions. And as the film played over and over again, Samantha watched with a satisfied expression on her face.

"So, is that the bitch you occupied your time with while I was gone?"

Terry couldn't believe that Kayla had fallen right back into Dareon's clutches. The betrayal felt like a ton of bricks sitting on his chest. He didn't realize he had fallen so hard until he had watched *his girl* being fucked by her ex-boyfriend. And if that ex had not been his cousin, he would have put a bullet through that nigga's head. Unable to control himself, Terry pulled out his Glock and fired two shots into the TV. The TV shot sparks, and then there was total blackness. Unmoved by his show of emotion, Samantha stepped from her position and carefully took the weapon from his hand. *Like taking candy from a baby.*

"If she fucked her boyfriend's cousin, why would you think that bitch wouldn't do the same thing to you? No one has ever loved you like I do, baby."

Samantha let her words sink in and awaited a response that did not come. Tired of waiting, she grabbed Terry's hand.

"Let's go home. I've missed you so much. I've prayed for this day when we would be reunited."

Samantha led Terry's hand to the nakedness beneath her skirt and across her wetness. She had lay awake many nights, wanting to feel him inside of her. No man had ever made her feel the way she did while with Terry, and she had beaten herself up over her addiction time and time again. The busted lip and black eye he had given her were minimal compared to the mental and physical abuse she had endured on the streets.

"Only you can get it this wet, daddy," Samantha whispered into Terry's ear. Even though he had not said anything, she could feel the hardening through his sweatpants. And Terry hated to admit that her wetness was doing a number on his libido. Even after all of these years,

Samantha still turned him on. She had been the only other female, besides Kayla, that he had ever let near his heart.

"So you think that showing me this shit is all it takes to make me forgive you? You killed our son, Samantha, and I still want to kill your ass for that shit."

Terry grabbed Samantha's long black hair and pulled it back, exposing her neck. He wanted to be mad, but he also wanted to feel her again. Watching Kayla fuck Dareon had his head in all the wrong places, and he wanted, no, needed to take his frustration out on someone else.

Samantha secretly gloated when Terry trailed his tongue up her throat and to her lips. She didn't scream out when he bit her bottom lip hard enough to draw blood before kissing her. And when his fingers began to maneuver themselves in her wetness, she almost lost it. Her fantasies were coming true. *If I can just get him to make love to me, I can get him back,* she thought as she began to fumble for the drawstring on his sweatpants.

"Let's take this back to my house."

Terry pulled away from Samantha and led the way to his vehicle. He was glad that everyone had left and could not see his backward spiral. There was nothing good that could come out of fucking Samantha, but he couldn't resist finding out whether her pussy was as good as it had been back in their prime. *It isn't like Kayla isn't still fucking her ex.*

The ride to Terry's house was made in complete silence. Samantha knew the way by heart and couldn't help but to smile at the memories of picking out that very home. It had once been theirs, and she was hoping to get back into Terry's good graces. It made her all warm and tingly on the inside that he had kept their house and had not sold it and moved. *Ha, bitch! He kept my house,* she said to Kayla in her head.

When the house came into view, Samantha allowed a Cheshire grin to spread across her face. *I'm home.*

Terry had promised himself that, after Samantha, he would never fall in love again, and unbeknownst to him, until he watched Dareon fuck Kayla on film, Terry was in love with Kayla. Even after watching her fuck his cousin after she had lied about breaking things off, he still wanted to talk to her, just to hear any excuse, so he could forgive her. The whole ride to his house he thought about Kayla, but realized that he would never be able to forgive her. And on top of everything, he had been reunited with a ghost from his past that his dick didn't want to deny.

Even after being absent for all this time, her body still fascinated him. Samantha had the kind of body that most women wanted and that most men fantasized about: thick thighs, perfect perky breasts, a round ass, and ebony skin as smooth as satin. And within seconds of entering the house, she had let him know she still wanted him just as bad. He kept replaying Kayla's video in his mind. So when he saw the unwavering lust in Samantha's eyes, it worked magic on his ego. He didn't resist when she led him to the master bedroom.

When she had him completely unclothed, instead of riding his dick like she planned to do, Samantha couldn't help wanting to taste him. *It has been so long...*Coating his package in saliva, Samantha got on all fours, relaxed her tonsils, and took in as much of his dick as she could handle. Not stopping until she felt him tense up, Samantha sucked his dick until she felt warm cum cascade down her throat. Swallowing his load, Samantha came up for air as she traced the outline of Terry's body from his belly button up with her saliva. Kissing first his neck, then his chin, and then his lips, Samantha continued to kiss Terry as she mounted him. As they played a battle with their tongues, Samantha rode Terry like he was a champion stallion and didn't stop until they both climaxed seconds apart. Exhausted, Samantha rolled onto her stomach as she struggled to catch her breath. Not into stopping so early in the game, Terry mounted her from behind and tried to bang her back out in an effort to forget his frustration.

****

Kayla sped down I-10, barely able to control her breathing. She had been dialing Terry for the past four hours, and his phone was still going to voicemail. Kayla's stomach was in knots, and she knew that something had to be wrong.

The Houston city limits signs came into view, and Kayla pulled into Terry's driveway in record timing. Seeing that his truck was home, she breathed a sigh of relief, as she cautiously approached his doorstep. Not seeing the dogs or any of his henchmen as she rapidly approached the porch, Kayla raised her hand to knock on the front door. As her hand touched the door, it immediately flew open. *This is not like Terry. What if something happened to him?* Unable to breathe, Kayla tiptoed through the house, not wanting to make any noise, in case there was someone still in the home who wanted to cause harm. She knew that Terry lived a dangerous lifestyle, and her inner psyche screamed for her to turn around and run back to her car. Hearing muffled noises coming from the master bedroom, Kayla silently climbed the staircase and placed her ear to the door. Her heart thudded against her chest, and she tried to distinguish the noises that were coming through the door. And then she heard:

"Terry, I know you missed this shit. Kayla can't make you feel like this. Tell me it's still mine."

"Damn, Samantha. I'm about to cum."

It was like an out of body experience. Kayla pushed the door open with the palm of her hand. It took her eyes only a moment to adjust to the scene laid out in front of her. Terry was bare assed naked, eyes closed as he grinded in and out of who she assumed was Samantha. Samantha saw Kayla first, and, even in the darkness, Kayla could see the hint of a smile cross Samantha's lips. Before Kayla could even think to not react, she felt herself leap across the room and onto the bed. Throwing wild blows, Kayla could see Samantha diving, fingernails first, for her face. Kayla leaned back, out of her reach, and leaned forward with a left hook, knocking Samantha backwards. Before Kayla knew it, she had the woman by the hair and was slamming her head into the wall, as Terry struggled to pull her off.

Terry pulled Kayla off of Samantha, as Samantha threw cheap blows at the restrained Kayla. Kayla tried fighting Terry off as she struggled to get back to Samantha. Sliding out of his grasp, Kayla ran and tackled Samantha. Just as she was about to slam her head into the floor, Terry again pried her off, this time flipping her over his shoulder so that she could not escape. Terry whistled and his dogs came out of nowhere, signaling them to sit in front of his bedroom door, locking Samantha in. Grabbing a pair of shorts out of his dresser, Terry cursed repeatedly as he packed a kicking and screaming Kayla up the stairs and into a guest room. He dumped Kayla on the bed and slammed the guest bedroom door behind him. Struggling to catch his breath, Terry slid on the pair of shorts, rested his hands on his knees, and glared at a very winded Kayla. Looking like a mad woman, she glared back, her shirt torn open and hair all over her head.

"Kayla, what the fuck is wrong with you?"

"What do you mean 'what the fuck is wrong with me'? I just caught my man fucking another female, and you ask what is wrong with me?" As Kayla spoke, she walked over to Terry, pointing her finger into his chest. "I have been calling your black ass all day, and, while I have been getting sent to voicemail, you have been entertaining that bitch."

Terry grabbed Kayla's wrist and pushed her backwards onto the bed.

"Get the fuck out my face, Kayla. And stop playing the fuckin' innocent ass role. I know you fucked Dareon."

Kayla paused and stared at Terry in disbelief. *How did he know?*

"So, what the fuck do you call this shit? You getting even? And you better not tell me that is the bitch on your neck? It better be....I'm telling you it better be another bitch named Samantha."

Terry's silence was enough to answer her question. Kayla went into a rage and began to throw wild punches in Terry's direction. He knew everything that she had been through, and he still lied and cheated on her with his ex. Terry had been playing games from the beginning. His supposed to be dead girlfriend was never even dead. That was probably the reason why he was never around to answer her calls, and she had been dumb and believed that he was always just handling business.

Terry grabbed Kayla's arms and pushed her on the bed.

"It's not what you think. I thought she was dead until today."

"So, you find out she's not dead, and your dick magically finds its way back into her. Do I really look that stupid?"

"Who I fuck is really none of your damn business? You have still been letting Dareon hit it, so I don't owe you shit."

Kayla wanted to kick and punch Terry, but he had her restrained in a tight grasp. *How could he know about*

Dareon? And Dareon was an accident. He was fucking his ex on purpose...

"I love you, Terry. I never meant to have sex with Dareon. It was an accident. How could you hurt me like this? I thought you cared about me."

Kayla, once again, found herself on the verge of tears.

"I saw the video. You weren't riding his dick like it was an accident."

"Someone sent my mother pictures of us together in Padre and in your hot tub. I was so mad that I went over there to confront him, and we got into a big fight. I was an emotional wreck, and it happened. I would never do anything to hurt you, but it doesn't matter, you have that bitch downstairs. I hate you!"

The tears escaped Kayla's eyelids and began to cascade down her cheeks. It didn't matter that she was sorry for fucking Dareon because Terry had his ex-girlfriend back in his life. She had seen the raw emotion in his eyes when he talked about Samantha, and there was no way that she could compete with that.

Terry tried wiping Kayla's tears with one hand while keeping her restrained with the other. That overwhelming desire to heal her heart from any pain resurfaced. He believed that she was sorry about fucking Dareon, but that still did little to alleviate the betrayal that he felt. And then there was the video. *Why would she let Dareon record her?*

"Kayla, look at me. Can I let go of your arms? And, baby, stop crying. You know I hate that shit."

Kayla nodded her head slowly but allowed the tears to continue to fall. She was tired of fighting, and how could he still call her baby when his true baby was just down the staircase?

"Why would you let him record you if it was an accident?"

Kayla looked at Terry with a stung expression on her face. *Wait! What? Dareon recorded us having sex.* It didn't take Terry long to put two and two together. Samantha had not just magically appeared with footage that was not even forty-eight hours old.

"Kayla, do you want to be with Dareon?"

Terry knew the answer in his heart, but he wanted to hear her say it. It was the only way that he could continue with what he had to say.

"No, I love you, Terry."

"Well, listen. Kayla, I didn't know Samantha was alive until today. She's the one that showed me the tape of you and Dareon. I fucked up by bringing her here, and I believe that you made a mistake. I need to figure out what's going on. Baby, do you trust me?"

Kayla wanted to scream out, "No! Fuck you! You are a cheating dog like the rest of them." Instead, her heart betrayed her, and she said, "Yes."

"Well, can you please leave? I promise you. I am going to make things right. Just leave, and let me handle things. I am going to have Chris come and pick you up. You can leave your car here. I don't want you driving in this condition."

"Why do I have to leave, Terry? And what about that bitch locked in your room?"`

"Kayla, trust me." Terry turned Kayla's eyes to meet his and wrapped her in his arms. "Kayla, I love you. Just please trust me." It was the first time that he had said those words since Samantha, and they felt foreign, but true, leaving his lips. Terry's sincerity prompted Kayla's need to confess.

"Terry, I have something I need to tell you."

Terry looked at Kayla not knowing what to expect.

"I'm pregnant, and I am pretty sure it isn't yours. I think I was pregnant in South Padre. Please don't leave me."

Terry put his head down in Kayla's bosom. *Could shit get any worse?* When he didn't answer after a few moments, he could hear Kayla begin to sob.

"Kayla, we are going to be okay. I love you, girl, and we will just deal with that once we get through this shit." Kayla could tell that it took everything in Terry for him to tell her that. She couldn't help kissing him repeatedly as tears ran down her face.

"Where's your phone? I need to call Chris to come and get you."

Kayla let Terry walk her outside and waited patiently while he called Chris to come and pick her up. Thankfully, Chris was in the area, so it only took minutes for him to pull up in front of Terry's house. Kayla could hear Samantha screaming Terry's name from inside the house, but he didn't leave her side until she was safely in Chris's vehicle.

****

"So, you still want that bitch, Terry, even after what I just showed you?" Samantha screamed out as Terry approached the bedroom.

Terry called his dogs off and opened the patio door for them to run outside. Ignoring Samantha for the moment, Terry commenced to trying to clean up his room that had been torn to shreds when Kayla had decided to wreak havoc. Stripping the linen from the bed and into a pile, Terry gathered the dirty laundry and dumped it down the laundry shoot for his maid, who came in daily to keep his home orderly.

"Help me clean this shit up," he instructed as Samantha stared at him in disbelief. *How dare he ignore me and ask for me to help like everything is okay?*

"Either help me fix this shit or leave." Terry looked at Samantha as he gave her his ultimatum. Not yet ready to leave without accomplishing her initial goal, Samantha threw on one of Terry's t-shirts to cover her nude body and helped him remake the bed with freshly laundered sheets. After picking up the clothes that had been tossed around the room, and restoring the pillows to their proper place, within a few minutes, Samantha and Terry had rid the room of any evidence of the disorder that had taken place only moments earlier.

"Now, can we talk, Terry?" Samantha pleaded as she followed him into the living room. "You can't love her more than you love me. I fucked up, but I am better now, and we can make this work."

As Terry sat on the sofa in the darkness, Samantha clutched his shirt close and took a seat directly next to him.

"Samantha, I love you. Look around. She ain't here, and you are. But tell me, how did you get that video?"

Samantha didn't want to tell Terry the truth, but she knew that lies would just piss him off even more. Hearing those words, Samantha leaned over and planted a kiss on Terry's lips and spilled her guts. As he kissed her back, he reached over and pulled her onto his lap. As she wrapped her arms around him, he held her like a baby and kissed the tip of her nose. "Get dressed. We have some moves that we need to make."

****

Kayla lay in Chris's guest room in the darkness, clutching her phone close, praying that Terry would hurry and call. Not knowing what to think or how she was supposed to feel, Kayla wrapped the comforter around her and rubbed her belly. Something was going to have to give, because all this stress and physical altercations couldn't be healthy for her unborn child. Not sure yet on whether or not she planned to keep the baby, she knew that she did not want to have a miscarriage before she made her decision.

"You okay, ma?" Chris asked as he peeked his head through the door.

Not getting an answer, he turned the light on and walked over to where Kayla lay with tears streaming down her face. These past few weeks had just been too much, even the sanest person would be on the verge of having a nervous breakdown.

"Kayla, this shit will all be over soon. And if it makes you feel any better, ya girls are on their way down here. Jordan called me and asked if I knew where Terry was since she couldn't get in contact with you, and, when I told her you were here, I couldn't talk her and Pharris out of coming."

Slightly relieved that her girls were on their way, Kayla closed her eyes. Sensing that she needed her rest, Chris leaned over and kissed her forehead before exiting the room. Terry was his boy, but, if he fucked this one up for Samantha's junkie ass, he had to be the biggest fool in the hood.

Chapter 17

Samantha and Terry quickly showered in separate bathrooms before they hurriedly got dressed. Since Samantha had not brought a change of clothes, Terry tossed her a pair of his old sweat pants, a t-shirt, and a hoodie before throwing on an almost matching ensemble himself. As Terry locked his house and set the alarm, he made a quick phone call while Samantha waited in the car.

"Chris, she a'ight?"

"Yeah, she straight, man. Just handle your business, and get back to your girl. I don't know how much more shawty can take, but Jordan and Pharris are on their way down here, so she will be taken care of."

Terry disconnected the call, and then eased into his SUV. Putting his vehicle into reverse, he adjusted the heat to combat the cool night air, and headed towards his old neighborhood. If anybody knew what he needed to do to be with the one he loved, it was his mother. Within minutes of leaving the house, Terry looked over at Samantha, who had let the seat back and dozed off.

Pulling up to the house he grew up in, Terry parked his large vehicle beneath the car port. After all the money that Terry had made in the streets, his mother still refused to move. Terry had her entire home remodeled, but that was all that he could do besides adding a security system to help protect his aging mother from the Fifth Ward streets, which had hardened over the years. While this had once been a working middle-class neighborhood, the product that Terry sold had helped to conquer many of a now lost generation.

Terry opened his door, and, after shutting it gently, he walked over to the passenger side and lifted a sleeping Samantha into his arms. As he used his key to enter through, first, the security bars, and, then, the front door, he tried his best not wake Samantha. Knowing that, at this early hour, his mother would be awake, Terry carried Samantha into his old bedroom, placed her under the covers, and then shut the door quietly behind him as he exited.

"Terrence!" He heard his mom call out from the kitchen as he smelled freshly brewed coffee.

"Yeah, it's me, Ma," Terry said as he walked into the kitchen and kissed his mom on her cheek.

"What brings you here so early, son?"

"I need to talk to you. It's about Dareon and Aunt Nicole, and I really don't know what to think right now."

With the mention of her sister's name, Priscilla Carver picked up her fresh cup of coffee and signaled her son into the living room. As Terry sat in his favorite arm chair, his mother took a seat on her plastic covered loveseat and prepared to answer her son's inquiries. It was long overdue that her sister's skeletons come out of the closet, and, if Nicole had messed with her son, Priscilla would do everything she could to aid in Nicole Anderson's fall from grace.

****

Kayla awoke to someone shaking her lightly.

"Kayla, we got here as fast as we could. What happened?"

Shielding her eyes from the blinding light that descended from the sparsely covered window, Kayla looked into her roommates' eager faces.

"What time is it?"

"Around eight. But you still have not answered our question. What happened to make you drive to Houston in the middle of the night?" Jordan asked as she sat on the edge of the bed.

Kayla yawned and proceeded to answer her roommates' questions. Starting at the point where her mother received the incriminating pictures in the mail, Kayla told her roommates everything that had happened, not leaving out any detail, including the one about her being pregnant. As she drew the tale of her traumatic last few days to an end, Pharris grasped her hand, struggling to close her gaping mouth.

"Why is all this happening to you?" Pharris asked out loud, not really expecting an answer.

For once, in what felt like a long time, Kayla did not burst into tears. As she looked at each of her roommates, she hugged them both and realized that she could not ask for better friends. In the middle of the night, both knowing they had class in the morning, her girls had driven four and a half hours to make sure that the third member in their trio was okay.

After crawling into the bed next to Kayla, Pharris adjusted her pillow.

"Do you need us to make room for you, too, Jordan?" Pharris asked, not bothering to turn around as she closed her already drooping eyes.

"No, I am about to go and talk to Chris," Jordan answered as she exited the guest room, softly closing the door behind her.

****

Armed with more information than he could muster, Terry left a sleeping Samantha over at his mother's house and headed over to Chris's. Pulling his truck into Chris's driveway, Terry used his key and entered. As he headed to the guest room where he knew Chris had placed Kayla, he was surprised to hear a female's giggles coming from the master bedroom. *I guess Jordan made it in,* Terry thought as he knocked lightly and opened the door to the guest room.

Lying in the bed, completely oblivious to Terry's entrance was both Kayla and Pharris, knocked out, asleep. Picking Kayla up, Terry carried her into the media room adjacent to the guest room, careful not to wake her.

"When did you get here?" Kayla mumbled as Terry kissed her forehead.

"Just now," Terry replied as he sat with Kayla in his arms on Chris's media room sofa.

"Why did it take you so long?" Kayla asked as she tried to open her tired eyes. She was glad that Terry was here and welcomed the sleep interruption.

Terry kissed each of her eyelids as he held her in his arms. *Damn, I love this girl.* Getting up to grab a blanket from the linen closet down the hall, Terry lay Kayla gently on the sofa. As he came back with the blanket, Terry removed his shoes and lay on the sofa behind Kayla, holding her close. Within a few minutes, Terry had joined Kayla in a peaceful slumber. After the drama of the night before and the trip to his mother's home that morning, Terry was long overdue for a few hours of sleep.

****

Where am I? Samantha awoke and glanced around her unfamiliar surroundings. As she pulled the covers off and adjusted the string on Terry's oversized sweatpants, she followed the scent of breakfast into the living room. As her eyes adjusted to the ancient living room décor, she immediately recognized where she was...*Terry's mother house.*

Little had changed about the room since she and Terry were in high school. Thinking back to countless hours she had spent making love to Terry in the same place she stood while his mother was at work, Samantha smiled to herself. Terry had always been the most passionate person she had ever made love to, and, as Samantha thought about the night before, minus her fight with Kayla, Samantha felt herself slightly moisten her borrowed sweatpants. *Thinking of Terry, where is he?*

"Hi, baby," Terry's mother said as she rounded the corner, careful not to startle Samantha. "Do you want breakfast?"

"No, ma'am, but do you by chance know where Terry went?" Samantha asked as she kissed what felt like her ex-mother-in-law on the cheek.

"I sure don't, Samantha," Mrs. Carver replied, eyeing Samantha carefully.

"May I use your phone?" Samantha asked as she ran her fingers through her long, now tangled hair, trying hard to think of any place where Terry might have been this time of the morning.

Mrs. Carver signaled Samantha into the kitchen and retreated into the arm chair where her son had previously sat to enjoy her breakfast and her soap operas. She knew where her son was, but there was no way she was telling Samantha anything. After the hell that Samantha had taken her son through, Samantha needed to be glad she had allowed her to sleep there.

Samantha dialed Terry's cell phone number. The phone rang five times and went to voicemail. On her fourth and fifth attempts, she slammed the phone down as she was sent to voicemail. *This motherfucker played me. He left me to be with that bitch.* Samantha retrieved her heels from Terry's old bedroom, and, with a slight wave, she walked out of his mother's home. Looking extremely odd in a pair of oversized sweats and stilettos, Samantha walked down the familiar street to the nearest bus stop. Although she had not been here in a while, these were some of the same streets Samantha had wondered when she was out to get her next fix.

After Terry had found out about her habit and began to hide his stash, Samantha had been forced to wander the seedy Houston streets to find a cure for her itch. Shivering at the thought of her days in the streets, Samantha placed her hood over her head and quickly got on the approaching bus. Not having a dime to her name, realizing she must have left her purse at Terry's, Samantha tossed the elderly bus driver a grateful smile as he waved her onto the half-empty bus without requiring a fare.

As Samantha sat on the bus, the wheels turned in her head as she thought about how she had been betrayed by Terry. He had filled her head with lies, just to get back to Kayla. Terry knew her all too well and knew that he couldn't have gotten rid of her without confessing his love. Clutching her nails into her fist so tightly she drew blood, Samantha hopped off at the next stop and walked down the block to the nearest pay phone. *Terry will pay…*

Chapter 18

Dareon rolled over out of his sleep and listened in disgust as Samara hurled repeatedly for what seemed like the hundredth time that morning. *This morning sickness shit is getting out of control.* Samara walked back into the bedroom after thoroughly brushing her teeth and lay back down, next to Dareon. As she reached over to wrap her arms around him, he hurriedly got out of the bed.

"It's time for you to go," Dareon said as he gathered her clothes and tossed them to her on the bed.

"What did I do this time, Dareon?" Samara asked as she crossed her arms and held her position in the bed.

Every time she turned around, he was putting her out, and she was just about fed up with his shit. Here she was, pregnant with his child. It was bad enough his sorry ass had not been to one doctor's appointment, but, every time he had a mood swing, he was putting her out of his condo. This time, she was not leaving. Sensing her mood and her stubbornness, Dareon grabbed Samara by her long blonde tracks and snatched her from his bed. As she hit the floor, he picked up the clothes he had recently placed on the bed and threw them at her, piece by piece. As each item hit Samara in her face, she just sat there and let the tears run down her face.

"Get the fuck out!" Dareon yelled as he laid back in the bed. Dressing quickly, Samara left Dareon's house with the slam of his door. This was not the first time he had put his hands on her, and probably would not be the last.

****

Kayla and Terry awoke to the sound of very loud laughter. Glancing at his cell phone, Terry looked at the time…*12:19 P.M.*…Wishing that he could sleep longer, but knowing that the racket downstairs was not about to stop anytime soon, Terry lifted Kayla from the sofa and gave her a kiss on her lips.

"Yuck! We need to brush our teeth," Kayla joked as she returned his gesture of affection.

"Oh, look! The love birds are up," Jordan said as she walked into the media room. "Kayla, I brought you some clothes, and a toothbrush and stuff."

Jordan handed Kayla a bag full of everything she needed to take a shower and get organized, and then headed back downstairs.

"There's food down here, too, if you guys want anything."

Kayla kissed Terry again, before heading into the nearest restroom. As Terry brushed his teeth with the extra toothbrush that thoughtful Jordan had bought, Kayla showered and then did the same. In the true fashion of Jordan, she must've went to the Galleria early that morning, because she had made sure Kayla had a designer outfit to start the day off right. Easing into a pair of Ralph Lauren Blue Label skinny jeans from the designer's new line and a coordinating Ralph Lauren Rugby tunic, Kayla brushed her hair into a ponytail. As Terry watched Kayla dress, he knew he had made the right decision in trying to save their relationship. Kayla was not only smart, but she was beautiful in his eyes.

As the couple walked into the kitchen together, Pharris couldn't help but smile at the glow she saw on Kayla's face. She didn't know whether it came from Kayla's pregnancy, or whether it was because Kayla was happy to be with her man. *Where is my man?* Pharris thought as she picked through the food on her plate.

As Kayla sat next to Pharris at the bar, Terry walked over to where Chris and Jordan were seated at the table, enjoying their late breakfast.

"You think you and Shon can handle things for a couple of days? I am going to go back to BR with Kayla," Terry asked Chris.

"Nigga, you know we straight. Handle your business," Chris said as he fed Jordan bacon off his plate.

Terry laughed to himself as he watched the two interact. He had never seen Chris so into any female before. Chris was usually the one in the crew who never dated, just talked to girls for a couple of months, and disappeared off of their radars. Not a heartbreaker, Chris just had never been one to hold on to a steady girlfriend, but, as Terry watched him and Jordan, he knew this case was going to be different.

As Kayla and Terry ate their fill of grits, eggs, bacon, and pancakes, the group chatted about nothing in particular. Pharris was going to follow Kayla and Terry back in Jordan's truck, while Jordan stayed in Houston a few days with Chris, since the semester was coming to a close and Jordan pretty much had finished the majority of her class work until finals. She didn't mind missing a couple of days of boring lectures to be with her new boo. Chris had promised to drive her back that weekend, when he came to pick up Terry.

After breakfast, Kayla, Pharris, and Jordan cleaned the kitchen as Chris and Terry went into Chris's office to discuss the business plans in Terry's absence. Unbeknownst to even Kayla, while Terry did plan to enjoy part of his time in BR, he had some family business that needed to be wrapped up, also. Terry was, also, pretty sure that sooner or later, he was going to have to deal with Samantha, now that she had picked the perfect time to rise from the dead.

Once the kitchen was spotless, with bags in hand, Kayla, Terry, and Pharris loaded into Jordan's Cayenne. They, first, went to Katy to pick up Kayla's car from Terry's house. Kayla waited in her car while Terry packed a bag and left instructions with his guards that he was not to have any visitors to his residence, besides Chris or Shon, in his absence. Within a couple of hours after leaving Chris's residence, the two vehicles were filled with fuel and headed back down I-10 to Baton Rouge.

****

As Kayla drove down I-10 towards Baton Rouge, she couldn't help but sneak irritated glances at Terry as he alternated between napping and answering his constantly vibrating phone. Pissed off at what she felt like was a lack of communication, Kayla couldn't help to be just as irritating, as she played loud obnoxious music to distract Terry from his sleep and his business calls.

"Kayla, why are you trippin'?"

"I'm not," Kayla replied as she switched lanes recklessly, causing the car behind her to swerve into the emergency lane. Ignoring the driver's repeated attempts to get Kayla's attention as he merged into the opposite lane, Kayla continued her high speed trek towards Baton Rouge.

"Kayla, slow the fuck down," Terry said as he shot her a warning glance from the corner of his eye.

"Do you want to drive?" Kayla shot back.

Deciding to ignore Kayla's obviously foul mood, Terry reclined the passenger seat and attempted to get a few more minutes of sleep before either his cell rang or Kayla turned the music back up.

Kayla stole a glance at Terry as she set her car to cruise control. *Damn! He looks cute sleeping.* Kayla placed her eyes back on the road as she crossed the Louisiana state line. Unconsciously drumming her fingernails against the steering wheel, Kayla chewed her bottom lip deep in thought. *I hate these mood swings. Terry is trying, but I am doing everything that I can to mess things up.* Kayla was suddenly jarred from her thoughts by a loud pop as her car spun out of control. Directing the car away from impending traffic as best as she could, Kayla screamed as the front of her Benz slammed into the cement guardrail, fiber glass shattering on impact as Kayla's three other tires seemed to burst simultaneously.

Terry popped up just as the airbag exploded in his face. As the car came to a sudden stop, Terry jumped from the passenger side and ran to the driver's side to help Kayla from the now smoking vehicle. As he approached Kayla's door, his knees turned into jelly as he observed her collapsed form suspended over the steering wheel.

"Shit! Don't do this to me," Terry begged as he opened the driver's side door, removed Kayla's seatbelt and carried his unconscious girlfriend from the severely mangled car.

In shock, Terry didn't even notice Kayla's very red blood staining his white t-shirt as he carried her down the emergency lane.

Pharris bobbed her head to Ciara's "Promise Remix" featuring R. Kelly as she tried to find the source of the impending traffic. As her eyes scanned the road ahead, she gasped as she recognized the crumbled form of what used to be Kayla's car resting head first against the barely scuffed cement guardrail. Pulling Jordan's Cayenne into the emergency lane, Pharris dialed the emergency operator as she hopped from the vehicle and ran towards the wreck. She gave the operator directions to the accident as she scanned the twisted metal for Kayla and Terry and tried to fight back tears as she realized the severity of the wreck. The entire front of Kayla's car was smashed in. The windshield was in the passenger area, and she could see that both airbags had been deployed. It only took Pharris a few glances past the smoldering mess to spot Terry crouched on the ground a few feet from the wreck with an unconscious Kayla clutched in his arms like a baby as he rocked back and forth.

Picking up her pace, Pharris hurried towards the two, her eyes fixated on Kayla's seemingly lifeless form. *Be strong. We need you.*

"Are you guys okay?" Pharris asked as she kneeled next to the couple. "I called the ambulance. Help is on the way."

As if waking from a daze, Terry stared through glazed eyes at Pharris. "I can't lose her," he said in a barely audible voice. Placing her hands on Terry's shoulders, Pharris looked into his eyes as the tears she fought back ran down her face.

"Kayla will be okay. My girl is a survivor."

As a stream of emergency officials and wreckers approached, Pharris wiped the dust from her jeans and brought her now weary form to its feet.

"Let me get Kayla's purse from her car. She'll need it when they get her to the hospital."

At the mention of hospital, Terry snapped from his daze.

"No. Stay here with Kayla. I will get the stuff out of the car," Terry said as he stared at the mangled mass of what used to be a luxury vehicle. As they swapped positions on the ground, Terry kissed Kayla on her forehead, careful to avoid her still bleeding gash before laying her across Pharris's lap. Terry sauntered over to the vehicle, threw open the passenger door, and retrieved his bag and Kayla's purse. Just as he was about to close the door, he couldn't help but notice a bulky manila envelope almost concealed behind the passenger seat. On a whim, Terry threw the envelope into his bag as he hurried over to where the paramedics were checking Kayla's vitals.

"Is my girl okay?" Terry asked as he approached the young medic working on Kayla.

"She unconscious, but her vitals are stable. We won't know more until we get her to the hospital. There is room for only one of you to ride," the medic said as he signaled from Terry to Pharris. "But we are taking her to the hospital in Lake Charles, the other can follow."

Terry glanced at the worried lines on Pharris's face, and the never ending flow of tears that cascaded down her face.

"You go," he told her. "Give me the keys to Jordan's truck, and I will follow."

Grateful for the gesture, Pharris took Kayla's purse from Terry's outstretched arm and handed him the keys to the Cayenne. Within seconds, the ambulance was headed down I-10, sirens blasting, as Terry followed close behind.

Chapter 19

Samantha, why couldn't you do something as simple as getting Terry away from Kayla? You need to be glad that I even sent the jet to pick you up after this fiasco." Nicole chastised as she cruised her rented Jaguar through the Baton Rouge International Airport terminal exit. "And look at you, what do you have on?"

Samantha glanced at Terry's oversized sweats as she attempted to wipe the fresh stream of tears from her already tear stained face.

"Only the weak cry." Nicole shot Samantha a look of pity as she entered onto the interstate. "You should have been crying when you let that skank take your man. You had everything in the palm of your fingertips..." Nicole's voice trailed off as she excelled the powerful vehicle towards the interstate. Samantha was young and naturally beautiful, something she had never been, but also very naïve, another character trait Nicole did not possess. Nicole could not, for the life of her, understand why the ones blessed in the looks area had to be so damned simple. It should have been a simple plan for a simple girl, yet Terry was still with Kayla. As Nicole approached the Mall at Cortana, she chose a spot near Macy's, which seemed to be the only suitable department store.

"Stay in the car," she instructed Samantha as she left the ignition running. *Bad enough I have to come to this mall filled with common people, but I'll be damned if I am seen anywhere with Samantha looking like she is still a crack whore.*

****

Terry paced back and forth in the waiting room as he and Pharris waited for any news on Kayla's condition.

"Terry, sit down. Wearing a hole in these people's carpet is not going to make anything happen sooner."

Finally deciding to take a seat, Terry turned to Pharris and asked, "What time are Jordan, Chris, and Kayla's parents supposed to get here?"

"They left as soon as I called them, and that was about an hour ago, so they should be here within the next hour and a half."

Terry placed his head in his hands. *This has been the craziest past couple of days of my life. If this isn't love, then I don't know what love is.* Terry smiled as the lyrics from one of the songs Kayla had played to annoy him what seemed like hours ago, resurfaced in his head. *What was the name of the song? Cupid's something...*

"Are you the family of Kayla Davis?" asked a handsome young doctor as he held out an outstretched arm, snapping Terry from his thoughts. "I'm Dr. Jakes."

As he shook the hands of both Terry and Pharris, Pharris couldn't help but let her hand linger a few seconds too long. *This man is gorgeous,* Pharris thought as she stared up into his brown eyes. Snapping back into reality, Pharris's solemn expression returned as she waited to hear the doctor's prognosis.

"Well, for starters, Kayla is a trooper. She suffered a nasty head injury, which we had to stitch up, but other than that, all her vitals are stable. We expect her to come to any moment now, but, be advised, she is going to have a nasty headache for a few days. We are going to try and keep her sedated, just to help alleviate the pain. You can both come back in about fifteen minutes to visit. I am just going to have her cleaned up."

Flashing Kayla's companions a mouthful of perfect white teeth, Dr. Jakes turned around to leave, and seemingly, as an afterthought, he spun around and spoke directly to Terry.

"Sorry. I forgot to mention this before. The baby is, also, doing just fine."

Pharris watched the doctor walk away. Through his white lab coat, she could see the muscles in his back as he sauntered down the hallway whistling gaily. *Not only is he fine, he seems happy,* Pharris thought, failing to hear Terry trying to get her attention.

"He's married. Did you not peep the ring?" Pharris heard when she finally broke from her daze.

"What?" she said as she whirled around to face Terry.

"Just kidding," Terry said, laughing. "I figured that would get your attention."

Not finding the joke funny at all, Pharris pushed Terry in his chest. "Punk, don't play with me. You know I need a man, especially after dealing with your married friend," Pharris said as she stuck her tongue out at Terry, unable to let him live down not detouring her from Shon's sorry ass.

Pharris had not even known that he was married until one night, out the blue, she received a call from none other than his wife. Laughing off the memory, Pharris again pushed Terry in his chest.

"You better stop hitting me before I get my girlfriend to kick your ass. You know she likes to fight," Terry said, laughing.

Pharris found herself laughing along with Terry. One thing she could definitely say was that, when it came to fighting, both Jordan and Kayla were down for whatever. The trio had gotten into a lot of shit together in what seemed like their short time as friends. Pharris took a seat next to Terry as the realization that she could have lost her friend hit her like a shock wave.

"I don't think life would have been the same if something would have happened to Kayla," Pharris told Terry as she rested her head on his shoulder.

"I know it wouldn't have," Terry replied.

"Take care of my friend, Terry. She deserves somebody good. Dareon has put her through so much, and all that she ever did was love him."

"That's my heart," Terry told Pharris as he suddenly rose to his feet. "But I need you to do something for me. Tell Kayla that I love her and that I will be back, but I need to go handle some business."

Pharris looked questioningly at Terry, but, when she saw the passion in his eyes, she knew that whatever he had to do had to be important for him to leave while Kayla was in the hospital.

"Be careful, and try to hurry back. You know how Kayla is."

Terry kissed Pharris on her forehead as he headed out the hospital exit. There were some things that needed to be handled, and there was no better time than now, so that, at least, when Kayla came home from the hospital, there would be no more drama.

Terry cruised down I-10 in Jordan's Cayenne as he tried to come up with a game plan on how he was going to handle what needed to be done in Baton Rouge. Pulling out his cell, he dialed the first person he knew for certain he needed to meet with.

“Who is this?” Dareon answered on the second ring. He was just leaving football practice, and the last thing that he felt like was any disturbances.

“Terry. We need to talk.” Terry listened to what seemed like an endless silence on the other end. Finally, Dareon spoke up.

“About what? Kayla’s your girl now, ain’t she? So what the fuck me and you have to talk about?”

“This shit is bigger than me and Kayla. Just be at your place when I get to Baton Rouge.”

Terry disconnected the call, not giving Dareon a chance to answer. He knew that Dareon would be there, just like he knew that, as soon as he disconnected the call, Dareon was going to call his Aunt Nicole.

****

“Ma, Terry’s on his way over here. I take it that Samantha delivered the package?” Dareon said within minutes of his conversation with Terry.

Confidence oozed from his voice as he waited for her response.

“She delivered the package, but don’t be fooled by your cousin’s antics, he is still playing house with your little floozy,” Nicole said while getting a pedicure at Baton Rouge’s Aveda Spa.

“So, where is Samantha?” Dareon asked un-amused at the fact that she had messed up the perfect scheme. All beauty, no brains, the kind of girl Terry needed.

“In the hotel room, sulking. Let’s just hope that she doesn’t go looking for another crack pipe, since that seems to be the only thing she was successful at,” Nicole replied as she laid her head back and enjoyed the feel of the paraffin wax being applied to her feet. “Son, call me when he arrives.”

After Dareon disconnected the call from his mother, he laid on his bed in deep thought. *What could Terry want that is so urgent?* As all kinds of thoughts raced through his head, Dareon could feel his eyes begin to droop, and, before long, he was snoring peacefully.

****

Terry cruised into Baton Rouge, as he merged onto the Dalrymple exit to the LSU campus. As he took the scenic route through the LSU campus, he processed what he planned to say to Dareon in his head. Armed with the information that his mother had supplied him with, he knew that this conversation could go one of two ways, either real bad or really-really bad.

As he turned into Dareon's parking garage, he braced himself for the worst while trying to prepare for the best. This was family, but, if need be, Terry was prepared for whatever. Removing the manila envelope from his bag, Terry parked and headed towards the nearest elevator.

Terry found Dareon's apartment on a hunch, considering he had not been to visit his cousin in over a year. He knew what floor and the general area, but he must admit, the LSU football décor and muddy sneakers outside the door aided him in finding the right apartment number. Terry raised his fist and knocked three times.

"Who is it?" Dareon called out clearly irritated and partially asleep.

"Terry."

Terry saw a light flick on from underneath the door, and then a bolt or two turn before the door flew open. Blocking the doorway, Dareon stood wearing nothing but a pair of sweatpants that he had pulled up to his knees. Terry brushed past Dareon and into the living room, ignoring his attempts to appear threatening. This was the same kid he used to bully growing up, and, even though they were older, there was still no doubt in Terry's mind that he could handle Dareon if the need arose. Growing up in the streets, Terry knew how to handle himself, and it would take a lot more than a few years of college football and weights to even make Dareon slightly intimidating in Terry's eyes.

"So, you wanted to talk. What's up?" Dareon said as he perched on a bar stool a few feet away from Terry.

"Did you ever wonder why it pissed your mother off so bad when she found out that Kayla was my girl?" Terry asked Dareon as he looked him square in the eyes. When Dareon didn't answer, Terry continued. "Look at what all she has done to keep me and Kayla apart. Didn't it occur to you that, maybe, there was a reason she didn't want Kayla with me, in particular?"

"That's my mother, man. She would have gone through all this shit, if it was another nigga in the family, too. Family doesn't fuck over family," Dareon said, emphasizing the last sentence for Terry to hear loud and clear.

"Let me guess. That's the bullshit she fed you."

"Watch your tone. That's my mother you talking about."

"The same mother who would stoop so low that she would send my ex-girlfriend with a tape of her son fucking my current girlfriend. That's some classy-ass shit. I have to give it to Aunt Nicole, though. She knows how to make a nigga hurt. But you know what they say, misery loves company."

Jumping off the stool, Dareon got in Terry's face.

"Watch what the fuck you say about my mother. Let's not talk about misery because, last I checked, doesn't your mother still stay in the ghetto?"

Before Terry could restrain himself, he punched Dareon in the jaw. As Dareon tried to recover, Terry had to stop himself from throwing another blow.

"My mother chose not to live a lie," a pissed off Terry replied. "And since this conversation is not going anywhere, why don't you call your mother and ask her why she chose to help everyone in the family but my mother? Why don't you ask her why the only time she speaks to her own sister is once a year at the family reunion? How about you ask her why she never allowed you to spend the night at my house growing up, even though I knew you would cry when I left?"

As Dareon sat on the sofa, clutching his jaw, childhood memories began to resurface. Growing up, the only time he had been allowed to see Terry was on holidays, and it would always be his Aunt Priscilla dropping Terry off and then leaving, not even coming into the house to say hello. He could remember begging his mother to go and spend the night at Terry's house, but was always told no because Terry stayed in the ghetto.

As Terry watched Dareon contemplate over his questions, he decided now was a better time than any to put closure to these unanswered questions and release this skeleton from the family closet.

"Do you ever wonder why we look so much alike Dareon?" Terry said as he walked over to where Dareon was seated. "Because we are not cousins. We're half-brothers."

Dareon looked up at Terry in disbelief. "That's bullshit. My father would have never cheated on my mother. He loved her."

"How would you know?" Terry asked, He was not surprised at Dareon's loyalty to his mother. "Since he is dead now, we will never really know, will we?"

Terry paused long enough to let his last sentence sink in before reaching into his pocket and pulling out a crumbled piece of paper. As Dareon took the paper from Terry's hand, and unfolded it to read the fine print, he could feel his perfect reality unfolding. There was no denying the information in his hand, it was Terry's birth certificate, and it bared his father's signature.

As if signaled by a judge to plead her case, Nicole walked in at the precise moment that Dareon was looking at Terry's birth certificate. Searching his mother's face for any sign of reason or remorse, Dareon looked up helplessly.

"You knew? The whole time, you knew?" Dareon said as he walked over to her holding the evidence. "This was not about me, the whole time you used me to destroy Terry and Kayla, and you were really trying to get back at my dad. He's dead, Mom. He's dead, and you can't change what happened in the past."

Nicole laughed at her naïve son. "Why would you think I ever cared that much about your dad? Men are the same. They lie and lie and lie. But my pretty little sister, getting everything handed to her as a child wasn't good enough. She had to get grown and sleep with my husband, too. And then here comes her son, he comes along and decides to steal your girlfriend. Can't you see what they are doing to this family? Nothing but backstabbers." Nicole shook her head in disgust as she spoke.

"You sick bitch," Terry said as he looked in her direction. "You fault everyone else for your mistakes. Tell the truth. My mother didn't try and steal your husband. He told you from the beginning he wanted to marry her. But then you came along and offered him the keys to success, the plan to start his business and all the connections he would need, if he just left my mother alone. But he didn't, did he? And you couldn't take it. Even after he married you, you still knew he would send my mother and me money, as long as she kept it a secret that he was my father. I grew up not knowing I had a father because of you, and because he was too greedy to do the right thing." Terry spat at his aunt.

"Awww, sob stories. Let me guess. Your mother told you that," Nicole said in her iciest tone.

Dareon grabbed Terry before he could leap over the sofa and grab Nicole by her neck. Unintimidated, Nicole adjusted the collar of her Marc Jacobs suit and took a seat at the bar.

"You vindictive bitch!" Terry yelled out as he struggled to break from Dareon's grasp and knock the smirk from Nicole's face.

"The little street boy has an extensive vocabulary," Nicole said as she beckoned Terry with her fingers. "And to think they always said public school education breeds an inferior class."

"Mother, enough!" Dareon shouted as he struggled, trying to control Terry. "You have done enough. Please leave."

Nicole looked from Dareon to Terry. "I know that you are not choosing the words of this lowlife and his slut of a mother over me," Nicole said to her only son.

"Leave!" Dareon shouted, reaffirming his last statement.

Glaring at her son in disbelief, Nicole gathered her composure. "You will regret this, Dareon," she said before exiting the apartment.

Upon her exit, Terry calmed down enough for Dareon to let him go.

"Man, I had no idea. I swear, I thought that she did this all for the family," Dareon apologized to Terry.

"Well, now you know. And do you know what's in this package?" Terry asked Dareon as he pointed to the manila envelope now on the floor by the couch.

"Naw," Dareon replied as he lifted the package to examine its contents. Inside of the bulky envelope were a DVD and a letter with a couple of printed sentences:

Every dog has its day. People should be more careful where they leave things lying around. You never know whose hands they could fall into.

-Samara

"Where did you get this shit?" Dareon asked Terry as he loaded the DVD player.

"It was lying in the back of Kayla's car." Terry shrugged as they both waited for the image to populate the screen.

Terry and Dareon both gasped as the picture began to play. Tied to the bed in the Hilton hotel was a naked Samantha as Nicole pleased her orally. Neither Terry nor Dareon could draw their eyes from the screen, as the homemade flick played, featuring Samantha and Nicole making love in every way possible. Clearly the dominator, Nicole went from orally pleasing Samantha to penetrating her with a ten inch strap on, while Samantha screamed and moaned in total ecstasy. As Dareon ran to the bathroom, trying to beat his wave of nausea, Terry continued to watch, as his mood alternated from fascination to disgust.

Terry changed clothes and showered at Dareon's house before heading back to Lake Charles to visit his girl in the hospital. Before he left, though, he had a sit down with Dareon and discussed everything with him, including the fact that Kayla was pregnant with his child. As Terry exited the condo, Dareon sat in the dark in utter disbelief. *Damn! I fucked up. Two girls pregnant at the same time.*

****

Terry arrived at the hospital to a small crowd gathered in the waiting room.

"Where have you been?" Jordan asked as she sat on Chris's lap, noisily chewing a piece of gum as she kept her eyes focused on the television ahead. A rerun of *Girlfriends* was on, and she hardly missed an episode.

"Handling some business. Where are Kayla's parents?"

"In the room with Kayla, where your black ass should have been," Jordan fussed as she kept her eyes glued to the screen.

"What room number?" Terry turned and asked Pharris, who was seated in the corner, trying her to best to stay out of the conflict. She knew how Jordan was, and, even though she had told Terry she would talk to Kayla for him, Jordan was another story.

"Room 610, down the hall to the left," Pharris replied as she tried to avoid eye contact. She hated being placed in the middle of conflict.

Terry headed down the hall, following the directions Pharris had given, and paused once he reached the door marked 610. His heart pounded. He didn't know what he was going to say. He had left the hospital to do the right thing, but he knew that now was neither the time nor place to talk to Kayla about all that had happened. As he rested his head against the door, it suddenly flew open, causing him to fly inside.

"Sorry about that, son." Mr. Davis said as he embraced Terry, followed by Mrs. Davis. "My daughter has been asking about you. Let me leave you two alone."

As the older couple exited the room, Terry walked to where Kayla lay with her head propped up. She was, also, watching *Girlfriends*.

"Where have you been?" she asked as she turned from the TV to look at him.

Terry grimaced at her bandaged forehead and tried not to recall the vivid images of her unconscious form when he had removed her from the car.

"We will talk about that later," he answered as he kissed her below the bandage. "How do you feel?"

"Ummm…let's see…like a bus hit me and then backed over me in reverse," Kayla replied as Terry tried to suppress a laugh.

One thing was for certain, she still had her sense of humor. Terry pulled a chair next to the bed and grabbed Kayla's hand.

"You know I love you, right?" he asked her as he looked into her hazel eyes.

"Yep," Kayla replied as she returned his intense gaze. "But can I ask you something?"

"Anything," Terry said as he continued to hold her hand.

"Would you leave me if I decided to keep this baby? I just feel like he or she has survived too much for me to even consider an abortion." Kayla stared into Terry's eyes.

Terry sat and thought for a few moments before finally replying. "No, Kayla, I would never leave you."

Epilogue

"What happened?" An almost hysterical Samantha asked as she heard Nicole enter the hotel suite that they shared. She had been in this room all day with no word from Nicole, no transportation, and no money. And worst of all, for the first time in two years, she was yearning for a hit.

Repeating her question as if Nicole had not heard, she plopped down in a leather recliner and waited for an answer.

"What happened is I trusted a stupid little bitch who can't do anything right. And by the way, what gave you the brilliant idea to vandalize Kayla's car? That is such low class, ghetto ho shit, if I ever saw any."

Even though Samantha was used to Nicole's verbal abuse, she refused to take the blame for something that she did not do.

"What are you talking about? I don't even know what that girl drives." Samantha struck back.

"Sure you don't." Nicole sarcastically replied as she removed her expensive garments and retreated to the oversized bathroom.

Following close behind Nicole, Samantha continued her assault of questions.

"What happened? Where is Terry? Is he still with Kayla?"

Irritated by her constant questions, Nicole lashed out, knocking Samantha to the cold, hard bathroom tile.

"Don't ask me anything, you ungrateful bitch. Yes, Kayla is still with Terry. And as a matter of fact, she is having his baby." Knowing that her last few words stung, Nicole smirked as she ran herself a steamy silk bath.

Unable to breathe, Samantha forced herself up from the bathroom floor. As tears streamed down her face, her last words fell upon deaf ears. "Don't worry, Nicole. I won't tell your secrets."

Seemingly in a daze, Samantha walked from the bathroom, through the tenth floor executive suite, and onto the balcony. All that she ever wanted was to show Terry that she had changed, and that she was sorry for killing their baby and getting hooked on drugs. All that she wanted was the only man that ever cared about her.

Her whole life, until she met Terry, she had searched for someone that could provide her with that love that she never got at home. An abusive father and a drunken mother had made her younger years hell, but, from the outside looking in, you never would have known that the beautiful girl who kept herself so together on the outside was breaking down on the inside. Not even bothering to wipe her runny eyes or nose, Samantha placed one foot over the balcony, and then the other.

As Nicole sat soaking in the sudsy water, mourning the lost love of her only son, she barely heard the faint scream or sickening thud of a despaired soul's last goodbye.

April

Kayla rested her head in Terry's lap as they sat at her apartment watching the NFL draft. As they announced the #10 pick, Dareon Anderson to the New England Patriots, Kayla and Terry both watched in silence as Dareon approached the stage. Not surprisingly, clutching Dareon's hand was a very pregnant Samara cutely clad in a Vera Wang original maternity dress. Gone were her long blonde tracks, replaced with a more sensible short blunt cut and bangs, which fit her small face.

Terry looked down at his pregnant girlfriend to test her facial reactions. It had only been a few months since her break-up with Dareon, and Terry knew that, even though Kayla would never admit it, to him, at least, she still had feelings for Dareon. And on top of that, she was also carrying his child.

Not one to judge, since he had his own demons, Terry accidentally let his mind drift to Samantha. He had found out about her suicide from Dareon, and even though he was in love with Kayla, for the second time in his life, he found himself mourning the death of his first love. Unable to sleep or eat for a couple of weeks straight, all that he kept thinking about was whether there was anything that he could have done to change the situation. Their last time together had left a bitter taste in his mouth, and all that he could do to lessen the pain was to force the memory of Samantha Janae Rogers from his memory.

One month less pregnant than Samara, Kayla was almost as big and had been warned by the doctor that if she didn't lay off on the ice cream and various other snacks she would suffer maternal obesity. Terry went to every doctor's appointment with Kayla, and they had found out only a couple of weeks earlier that Kayla was having a girl. Terry and she had agreed after much negotiation with Dareon, whom he now recognized as his half-brother, that their baby girl would grow up thinking that Terry was her father just to prevent any household confusion, since obviously Kayla and Terry were not breaking up anytime soon. Even though Dareon wanted Kayla back, he recognized his mistakes and decided to let her go and be happy with someone else. And since Samara was carrying his baby boy, even though he didn't love her, he would try to make things work for the sake of his child. Dareon and his mother had yet to mend their relationship.

As for the trio, Jordan was still dating Chris, and Pharris had even managed to find love. While Kayla was in the hospital, Pharris and Dr. Jakes had gotten extremely close and now made the commute to see each other every weekend. Whereas once the trio lived by the motto: Where is my man? They all now had one to claim as their own.

June 2006

Barely ninety-six pounds, starving, strung out, and broke, Samantha now stood in front of Nicole, asking for her help. Since she had met Nicole years earlier at one of the annual family reunions, she envied the woman. Unattractive in every sense of the word, but yet so poised and successful, Nicole was everything that Samantha had planned to be, before she allowed drugs to take over her life.

"I have nowhere to go. Please just help me," Samantha begged as she shivered like a rag doll in 103 degree weather.

"And why would I do that?" Nicole asked in disgust as she stared at the disintegrating figure of someone who used to be beautiful.

Through chattering teeth and with as much courage as she could muster, Samantha answered, "Because I know how your first husband really died. You know, sometimes, you can't just leave stuff lying around."

A Fashionable Revelation

(Coming Soon)

What kind of person have I turned into, and when did I allow my infatuation with Dareon to control my life? After all that my best friend endured, I allowed myself to tread within those same footsteps. Now, I am sleeping with my best friend's ex-boyfriend and laying everything on the line. So many nights I have cried, knowing that a decision that was initially made from pure lust, could be the same decision that causes my world to come crashing down around me.

Three long years, I watched the turmoil that Kayla endured at the same hands of a man who I can't seem to get enough of. I could never understand why she didn't just let it go. The nights that she cried on my shoulder and confessed the pain in her soul were not enough to deter me from following in her footsteps.

I have the boyfriend that I always wanted and unbeknownst to him, our relationship is based on a lie. The nights that he assumes that I am out late studying or simply calling it an early night are really nights that I spend letting Dareon stroke me from every angle imaginable.

I don't even know how this happened. The same man that I despised for the pain that my friend endured at his hands has seduced me to a point that I can't even recognize what's important. I love my best friend, I love my boyfriend, but I also love Dareon. But if there is one thing that life has taught me, what is done in the dark eventually comes to the light. And when it does, I risk losing everything.

Tonia the Author

Even though Tonia was born and raised in Houston, it was during her college years at Louisiana State University in Baton Rouge that *Fashionably Deceptive* began to manifest. Always an avid writer and reader, Tonia decided to try her hand at writing a novel based "loosely" around the lives, fantasies, and experiences of her college roommates. That idea would manifest itself into a masterpiece of a novel that will have readers hooked from start to finish.

Please visit her website at: www.toniatheauthor.com

Made in the USA
Charleston, SC
18 June 2013